I0657031

Henry Curties

The Queen's Error

Henry Curties

The Queen's Error

ISBN/EAN: 9783955630720

Auflage: 1

Erscheinungsjahr: 2013

Erscheinungsort: Bremen, Deutschland

@ Leseklassiker in Access Verlag GmbH, Fahrenheitstr. 1, 28359 Bremen. Alle Rechte beim Verlag und bei den jeweiligen Lizenzgebern.

Leseklassiker

Contents

Chapter I. A Strange Visit

I turned the corner abruptly and found myself in a long, dreary street; looking in the semi-fog and drizzle more desolate than those dismal old-world streets of Bath I had passed through already in my aimless wandering; I turned sharply and came almost face to face with her.

She was standing on the upper step, and the door stood open; the house itself looked neglected and with the general appearance of having been shut up for years. The windows were grimed with dirt, and there was that little accumulation of dust, pieces of straw, and little scraps of paper, under the two steps which tells of long disuse.

She stood on the step, a figure slightly over the middle height, leaning one hand on a walking stick, and her face fascinated me.

It was the face of an old lady of perhaps seventy, hale and healthful, with fresh colour on the cheeks, and bands of perfectly white hair falling over the ears. But it was the expression which attracted me; it was peculiarly sweet and winning.

My halt could only have been momentary. I recollected myself and was passing on, when she spoke to me.

"Would you be so kind as to do me a favour, sir?" she asked.

The voice was as sweet and winning as her expression; though she spoke perfect English, yet there was the very slightest *soupçon* of a foreign accent. Of what country, I could not tell.

I stopped again as she spoke, and having perhaps among my friends a little reputation for politeness to the weaker sex, especially the older members of it – for I am not by way of being a Lothario, be it said – I answered her as politely as I could.

"In what way may I be of service to you?"

She brought her walking stick round in front of her and leant upon it with both hands as she made her request. She then appeared, in the fuller light of the yellow-flamed old-fashioned gas lamp opposite, to be much older than I first thought.

"I want you, if you will," she said, "to come into this house for a few minutes. I wish to ask a further favour of you which I shall then have an opportunity of explaining, but, on the other hand, the service I shall ask will not go unrewarded."

Prepossessing though her appearance and address were, yet I hesitated.

I took another long look at her open face, white hair, and very correct old lady's black hat secured by a veil tied under her chin. It was just such a hat as my own dear mother used to wear.

"You seem to hesitate," she remarked, noting, I suppose, my delay in answering her; "but I assure you you have nothing to fear."

I took a sudden resolve, despite the many tragedies I had read of in connection with empty houses; I would trust her.

There was something about her face which conveyed confidence.

"Very well," I replied, "if I can be of any use to you, I *will* come in."

"Thank you," she said, "then kindly follow me."

She turned and held the door for me to pass in; when I was inside she closed it, and we stood almost in complete darkness, except for the glimmering reflected light of the yellow street lamp opposite, which struggled in through the dirty pane of glass over the door.

"Now," she added, "I will get a light."

She passed me and went to the hall table on which stood one of those candlesticks in which the candle is protected by a glass chimney. She struck a match and lighted a candle. "Now if you please," she added, going on before me down the dark passage. I saw now from her tottering walk that she was much older and much more feeble than I had imagined. I followed her and saw signs of dust and neglect on every side; the house, I should say, had stood empty for many years. But as I followed the old lady one thing struck me, and that was, that instead of the common candle which I would have expected her to use under the circumstances, the one she carried in its glass protector was evidently of fine wax. She took me down a long passage, and we came to a flight of stairs leading to the kitchens, I imagined.

"We must go down here," she announced. "I am sorry to have to take you to the basement, but it cannot be helped." Again I had some slight misgivings,

3

but I braced myself. I had made up my mind and I would go forward.

I followed her as she went laboriously step by step down the flight. At the bottom was the usual long basement passage, such as I expected to see, but with this difference, it was swept and evidently well kept.

The old lady led on to the extreme end of this passage towards the back of the house, then opened a door on the left hand and walked in. At her invitation I followed her and found her busily lighting more wax candles fixed in old-fashioned sconces on the walls. As each candle burned up I was astonished to find the sort of room it revealed to me.

It was a lady's boudoir beautifully furnished and filled with works of art; china, choice pictures, and old silver abounded on every side; on the hearth burned a bright fire; on the mantelpiece was a very handsome looking-glass framed in oak. My companion, having lit six candles, went to the windows to draw down the blinds. I interposed and saved her this exertion by doing it myself.

I then became aware that the house, like so many others in Bath, was built on the side of a hill, the front door being on a level with the street, whilst the lower back windows even commanded lovely views over the beautiful valley, the town, and the distant hills beyond.

Below me innumerable lights twinkled out in the streets through the misty air, while here and there brightly lit tram cars wound through the town or mounted the hills. Thick though the air was the sight was exceedingly pretty.

I could now understand how even a room situated as this was in the basement of a house could become habitable and pleasant. The voice of the old lady recalled me to myself as I pulled down the last blind.

"I am sorry to have to bring you down here," she said. "It is hardly the sort of room in which a lady usually receives visitors, but you will perhaps understand my liking for it when I tell you that I have lived here many years."

The information surprised me.

"Whatever induced you to do that?" I asked without thinking, then recollected that I had no right to ask the question. "You must excuse my question," I added, "but I fear you find it very lonely unless you have some one living with you?"

"I live here," she replied, "absolutely alone, and yet I am never lonely."

"You have some occupation?" I suggested.

"Yes," she replied, "I write for the newspapers."

This piece of information astounded me more than ever. I imagined it to be the last place from which "copy" would emanate for the present go-ahead public prints, and the old lady to be the last person who could supply it.

She saw my puzzled look, and came to my aid with further information.

"Not the newspapers of this country," she added, "the newspapers of – of foreign countries."

I was more satisfied with this answer; the requirements of most foreign journals had not appeared to me to be excessive.

"I too am a brother of the pen," I answered, "I write books of sorts."

The old lady broke into a very sweet smile which lighted up her charming old face.

"Permit me to shake hands," she suggested, "with a fellow-sufferer in the cause of Literature."

I took her hand and noted its soft elegance, old though she was.

She crossed to a carved cupboard which was fixed in the wall, and took from it a tiny Venetian decanter, two little glasses, and a silver cigarette case.

"We must celebrate this meeting," she suggested with another smile, "as disciples of the pen."

She filled the two little glasses with what afterwards proved to be yellow Chartreuse, and held one glass towards me.

"Pray take this," she suggested, "it will be good for you after being out in the damp air."

I took the tiny glass of yellow liqueur in which the candlelight sparkled, and sipped it; it was superb.

"Now," she continued, indicating an armchair

on the farther side of the fireplace, "sit and let us talk."

I took the chair, and she opened the silver box of cigarettes and pushed them towards me.

"I presume you smoke?" she suggested. "I smoke myself habitually; I find it a great resource and comfort. I lived for a long time in a country where all the ladies smoked."

I took a cigarette, lit a match, and handed her a light; she lit her cigarette with a grace born of long habit.

"Now," she said, as I puffed contentedly, "I can tell you what I have to say in comfort."

I certainly thought I had made a good exchange from the raw air of the street to this comfortable fireside.

"It will not interest you now," she continued, "to hear the reasons which have moved me to live here so long as I have done; that is a story which would take too long to tell you. All the preamble I wish to make to my remark is this; that the favour I shall ask of you is one that you can fulfil without the slightest injury to your honour. On the contrary it will be an act of kindness and humanity which no one in the world could object to."

"I feel sure of that," I interposed with a bow, "you need not say another word on that point."

I was really quite falling in love with the old lady, and her old-world courtesy of manner.

"I will then come straight to the point," she proceeded, taking a curious key from her pocket; it was a key with a finely-wrought handle in which was the letter C.

"I want you to open a secret drawer in this room, which, since its hiding-place was contrived, has been known only to me and to one other, the workman who made it, a Belgian long since dead. Please take this key."

I took it.

"Now," she continued, "cast your eyes round this room, and see if you can detect where the secret safe is hidden."

I looked round the room as she wished, and could see nothing which gave me the slightest clue to it.

"No," I said, "I can see nothing which has any resemblance to a safe."

She laughed, and, rising from her seat, turned to the fireplace and touched a carved rose in the frame of the handsome over-mantel; immediately the looking-glass moved up by itself in its frame, disclosing, apparently, the bare wall.

"Please watch me," proceeded the old lady.

She placed her finger on a certain part of the pattern of the wall paper beneath, and the whole of that part of the pattern swung forward; behind was a safe, apparently of steel, evidently a piece of foreign workmanship.

"Please place the key in the lock, and turn it," she asked, "but do not open the safe."

I regarded her proceedings with much interest, and rose from my chair and did as she asked.

"Thank you," she said, when she heard the lock click and the bolts shoot back, "now will you lock it again?"

I did so.

"Now please put the key in your pocket, and take care of it for me. I give you full authority to open that safe again in case of necessity."

"What necessity?" I asked.

"You will discover that in due course," she answered.

This was about the last thing I should have expected her to ask, but nevertheless I did as she told me and put the key in my pocket.

"Please notice how I close it again," was her next request.

She pushed back the displaced square of the wall paper pattern, which was simply the door of a cupboard. It closed with a snap and fitted so exactly into the pattern of the paper that it was impossible to detect it.

Then with a glance towards me to see that I was paying attention, she touched a carved rose on the frame of the over-mantel on the opposite side to that which had caused the looking-glass to move, and at once the latter slowly slid down again into its place.

I stood gazing at her as this was accomplished, and she noted the look of inquiry on my face.

"There is only one thing now I have to ask you," she said, "and then I will detain you no longer. Will you oblige me by coming to see me here at five o'clock to-morrow?"

I considered for a moment or two, and then recollected that there was nothing in my engagements for the next day to prevent my complying with the old lady's request. My life for the last week had been occupied in taking the baths and the waters at regular intervals, with the daily diversion of the Pump Room concert at three.

"Yes," I answered, "I shall be very pleased to come and see you again at five to-morrow."

Although up to now I looked upon her proceedings as simply the whims of an eccentric old lady, yet I felt some considerable interest in them.

"Then let me fill your glass again with liqueur?" she suggested. Alluring as the offer was I declined it.

I buttoned up my overcoat and prepared to depart, accepting, however, the offer of another cigarette.

The old lady insisted upon accompanying me to the door, and went on in front with a candle, despite my remonstrances, to show me the way upstairs.

She had one foot on the stair when she stopped.

"Do you mind telling me your name?" she asked.

I handed her my card, and she put up her glasses.

"'William Anstruther,'" she read. "That is a coincidence." "I had nearly forgotten one thing," she continued. "I must give you a duplicate latch-key to let yourself in with. I have a habit of falling asleep in the afternoon, and you might ring the bell for half an hour and I should not hear you."

She went back into the room we had left and returned in a few moments with the latch-key, which she gave me.

Despite my endeavours to persuade her, she went with me to the front door, and I felt a deep pity for her when I left, thinking that she was to spend the night alone in that dismal old house.

"*Au revoir* until five to-morrow," I said cheerfully, as I bowed and left her.

She smiled benignantly upon me.

"*Au revoir*," she answered.

When the door had closed and it was too late to call her back, I recollected one piece of forgetfulness on my part; I had never thought to ask her name!

Chapter II. The Man with the Glass Eye

I took a note of the number of the house – it was 190 Monmouth Street – and gazed a little while at its neglected exterior before I walked away into the mist towards my hotel.

Over the whole of the front windows faded Venetian blinds were drawn down; it was one of those houses, sometimes met with, shut up for no apparent reason, and without any intention on the part of the owner, apparently, to dispose of it, for there was no board up. It was not until later that I learned that the house belonged to the old lady herself.

I returned to my hotel, that luxurious resort of the wealthy and rheumatic, its well furnished interior looking particularly comfortable in the ruddy glow of two immense fires in the hall. I had left it early in the afternoon, before the lamps were lit, tired of being indoors; the change was most agreeable from the damp, misty atmosphere without.

I betook myself to the smoking-room, and, being a lover of the beverage, ordered tea, with the addition of buttered toast. Delighted with the big glowing fire in the room, and believing myself to be alone, I threw myself back luxuriously into a big, saddle-bag chair.

As it ran back with the impetus of my descent into it, it jammed into one behind, and from this immediately arose a very indignant face which looked into mine as I turned round. It was a dark, foreign-looking face, the red face of a man who wore a black moustache and a little imperial, and whose bloodshot brown eyes simply *glared* through a pair of gold-rimmed pince-nez. There was something very strange about these eyes.

"I really beg your pardon," I said. "I didn't know you were there!"

The fierce expression of the bloodshot eyes changed to one of somewhat forced amiability.

"Pray don't apologise," he answered, with just the merest touch of a foreign accent in his voice, that sort of undetectable accent which some men of cosmopolitan habits possess, though they are rarely met with.

"I think I must have been asleep," he added, "and the little shock awoke me from a disagreeable dream. There is really so little to do in this place besides bathing and sleeping."

"And water drinking," I suggested, with a smile.

"I do as little of that," he answered hastily, with a grimace, "as I possibly can. By the bye though," he continued, wheeling round his chair sociably beside mine, "do you know that the Bath water taken *hot* with a good dash of whisky in it and two lumps of sugar is not half bad?"

I took a good look at his face as he sat leering at me through his glasses. From the congested look of it, I could quite believe that he had sampled this mixture, or others of a similar alcoholic nature, sufficiently to give an opinion on the point; his bloodshot eyes also testified to the fact.

But concerning these latter features, the reason

of the curious look about them was solved by the firelight; one of them was of glass! I saw that it remained stationary whilst the other leered round the corner of the gold-rimmed pince-nez at me. It was a very good imitation, and was made *bloodshot* to match the other.

My tea and buttered toast arrived now, and I made a vigorous attack upon the latter.

"The idea of mixing whisky with Bath water," I replied, laughing, "never struck me. It appears novel."

"I can assure you," continued my new acquaintance, "that many of the old men who are ordered here to Bath do it, and I should not be surprised to hear that it is a practice among the old ladies too. Look at their faces as they come waddling down to table d'hô´te!"

This appeared to me rather a disrespectful remark with regard to the opposite sex, and I answered him somewhat stiffly, "I hope you are deceived."

He was not a tactful person by any means: he made an observation then concerning my tea and buttered toast.

"I really wonder," he said, "how you can drink that stuff," with a nod towards my cup. "It would make me sick; put it away and have a whisky and soda with me?"

I naturally considered this a very rude remark from a perfect stranger.

"I am much obliged," I snapped, "but I prefer tea."

At that moment I put my hand in my pocket for my cigarette case. I thought I would give this man one to stop his tiresome talking; as I pulled it out the key of the safe which the old lady had given me fell out with it. Before I could stoop and pick it up myself the man with the glass eye had got it. He put it up close to his good eye and examined it critically. "What an extraordinary key!" he observed. "Where did you get it?"

Then he saw the letter C which was worked among the elaborate tracery of the handle, and he became greatly agitated.

"Where did you get this from?" he repeated abruptly.

I did not answer; I got up from my seat and took the key out of his hand; he was by no means willing to part with it.

"Excuse me," I said.

Then with the key safe in my pocket and my hand over it, I walked out of the smoking-room, leaving behind me two pieces of buttered toast and perhaps a cup and a half of excellent tea all wasted.

I am a delicately constituted individual, and I preferred smoking my cigarette all alone in a corner of the big hall, to consuming my usual allowance of tea and buttered toast in the society of the glass-eyed person in the smoking-room. I considered that I was doing a little intellectual fast all by myself.

I saw nothing more of my friend of the false brown optic that evening, except that I observed his bloodshot eye of the flesh fixed scathingly upon me from a remote corner of the great dining-room, where he appeared to be dining mostly off a large bottle of champagne.

I sauntered away my evening as I had done the others of my first week's "cure" in Bath, making a fair division of it between the dining-room, the smoking-room and the reading-room. I did not go near the drawing-room; its occupants consisted solely of a few obese ladies of the type referred to by the gentleman with the glass eye, wearing such palpable wigs that my artistic susceptibilities were sorely wounded at the mere sight of them, and my sense of decency outraged.

I went to bed in my great room over-looking the river and the weir, and I lay awake listening to its rushing waters, for the night was warm and almost summer-like, as it happens sometimes in a fine November, and my windows were open.

I suppose I fell asleep, for when I was again conscious, the Abbey clock struck four; at the same moment I became aware that some one was in my room. I could discern the figure of a man in the shadow of the wardrobe near the chair on which I had placed my clothes when I took them off. I leant over the side of the bed and switched on the electric light; the figure turned. It was the dark man with the glass eye!

"What the devil are you doing in my room?" I asked in none too polite a tone.

He was not at all disconcerted, but stood looking at me, replacing his pince-nez.

"Well, really," he replied, "wonders will never
cease. I thought I was in my own room!"

I knew he was lying.

"I fail to perceive," I said, sitting up in bed, "in
what manner you could have mistaken this room for
your own. In the first place the door is locked."

"Just so," remarked my visitor, "that's exactly
where it is; I came in at the window."

"The window?" I repeated.

"Yes, the window. I couldn't sleep, so took a
stroll up and down the balconies, and when I returned to my room, as I thought, I came in here by
mistake."

The excuse was plausible, but I didn't believe a
word of it. I was in a dilemma, and sat scratching my
head. I could not prove that the man was lying, and
therefore had to take his word.

"Very well, then," I said in a compromising
tone, "having made the mistake, and it being now
nearly five, perhaps you will be able to find your
way back to your room and go to sleep."

I thought I was putting the request in as polite a
manner as possible, and I expected him to move off
at once.

He did nothing of the kind. With a quick movement of his hand to his hip, he produced a revolver
and covered me with it.

"Where's that key?" he asked.

He took my breath away for a few moments and I couldn't answer him, then I regained my presence of mind.

"What key?" I asked, though I had a pretty shrewd idea as to the key he wanted.

"The key which dropped out of your pocket this afternoon."

"I don't keep it in bed with me," I replied. "I'll get out and fetch it for you, you are quite welcome to it."

I temporised with him, but I was perfectly determined in my own mind that he should never have it while I lived.

I slipped out of bed and he still held the pistol pointed towards me but in a careless way. I think he was thrown off his guard by my apparent acquiescence.

The clock of the Abbey struck five and he involuntarily turned his head at the first stroke; in that moment I made a sweeping blow with my left arm and knocked the revolver out of his hand; it fell with a crash on the floor. Then I seized him by the throat and tried to hold him. He was, however, like an eel; he wriggled himself free and struck me a heavy blow on the chest which sent me backwards, then he turned and darted towards the window, but as he did so I heard something fall on the floor. For one second his hand went down on the floor groping for it, then, with a curse, he snatched up the revolver, which lay near, and darted out of the window on to the balcony. It all occurred in a few moments, and I followed him as quickly as I could, but when I reached the window I saw him flying along the balcony; he had already cleared several of the little divisions railing off one apartment from another, and I could see it would be useless to follow him.

As I turned and re-entered the bedroom something lying on the floor caught my glance and I stooped and picked it up.

It was the man's glass eye, it had dropped out!

"Now," I said to myself, surveying the blood-shot counterfeit orb as I held it under the electric light. "*Now* I shall be able to trace him by means of his missing eye and hand him over to justice."

I was fated to be disappointed.

Late the next morning when, having passed the remainder of the night sleeplessly, I came down the main staircase into the hall, almost the first person I met was my friend of the glass eye coming in at the front door. He had apparently just left a cab from which the hotel porters were removing some luggage. He came straight to me, and, looking me in the face, had the impudence to bid me "Good morning."

"Went over to Bristol last night," he explained, "for a ball, and have only just got back. Had awful fun!"

I returned his look for some time without speaking; he had another glass eye stuck in which was the counterpart of the other. I saw now clearly that he had two or more glass eyes for emergencies.

"Bristol!" I repeated. "Did you not come into my room last night and – – ?"

"And what?" he asked innocently.

"And threaten me?" I added.

He seemed highly amused.

"Do you mean before I went?" he asked.

"No, about four o'clock this morning."

This time he burst out laughing.

"My dear fellow," he said with impertinent fa-miliarity, "at four o'clock this morning I was dancing like mad with some of the prettiest girls in Bristol!"

Liar! It was on the tip of my tongue to ask him whether his glass eye had fallen out during his terp-sichorean efforts! It was, however, perfectly evident to me that he intended to deny that he had been in the hotel during the night, and probably had had time to establish some sort of an *alibi*. I therefore decided to move cautiously in the matter.

I turned on my heel and went into the dining-room to breakfast without another word.

But I made it my business during the morning to inquire of the hall porter, who I found had been on duty up to eleven o'clock on the previous night, whether Mr. Saumarez – for that I discovered was the name he had entered in the hotel visitors' book – had left the hotel on the previous evening.

The porter unhesitatingly informed me that he

had to go to a ball at Bristol!

Really, when I left this man I began to wonder whether I had been dreaming, until I recollected the glass eye which was securely locked up in my dressing-case, such things not being produced in dreams and found under the pillow in the morning wrapped in an old telegram as this had been.

I went next to the chambermaid who presided over the corridor in which Mr. Saumarez' room was.

Being a good-looking girl I gave her half-a-crown and chucked her under the chin.

"Look here, Maria," I said, "just tell me whether 340, Mr. Saumarez, was in or not last night. I'm rather curious to know and have got a bet on about it with a friend."

She looked at me knowingly and giggled.

"Why, *out*, sir, of course," she replied; "he came in at half-past ten this morning with his boots un-blacked. We all know that *that* means."

This evidence to me appeared conclusive. I gave the chambermaid a parting chuck under the chin – no one being about – and dismissed her.

Then, it being a fine morning, I went out for a walk.

I went right over the hills by Sham Castle and across the Golf Links, being heartily sworn at – in the distance – by sundry retired officers for not getting out of the way. But I was trying to have a good think over Mr. Saumarez, his duplicate glass eyes, and the reason why he wanted the key of the old lady's safe.

I so tired myself out with walking and thinking, with no result, that when I got back and had lunched late all by myself in the big dining-room, I went into the smoking-room, which this time was quite empty, and fell asleep in front of the great fire.

My sleep was curiously broken and unrestful, and full of that undefined cold apprehension which sometimes attacks one without any apparent reason during an afternoon nap.

I awoke at last to hear the old Abbey clock striking five, and then I nearly jumped out of my seat, for I recollected my promise to the unknown old lady in Monmouth Street to visit her again that day at that very hour.

I hurried through the hall to the coat room, and, seizing my hat, rushed out and just caught a tram which was gliding past in the direction of the upper town where Monmouth Street stretched its length along the slope of the hill.

It was only three minutes past five when the gaily lighted tram deposited me at the end of my old lady's street, and I set off for Number 190, which was at the other extremity of the long, badly lighted thoroughfare, looking, with its interminable rows of oblong windows, like an odd corner of the eighteenth century which had been left behind in the march of time.

I found the house practically as I had left it; there was no fog that evening, and I had a better opportunity of observing its general appearance in the yellow flare of the old-fashioned gas lamp opposite.

The house on one side of it was to be let, with a large staring board announcing that fact fixed to the railings; the house on the other side was a dingy looking place with lace curtains shrouding the dining-room windows and a notice outside concerning "Apartments."

I drew out the latch-key, blew in it to cleanse it from any dust, then, with very little difficulty, opened the door and entered Number 190.

Chapter III. The Second Visit and its Result

The first thing which caught my attention was the wax candle with its glass shade standing on the raised flap which did duty for a hall table.

I at once lit the candle from the box of matches by it, and then, when it had burned up a little, proceeded at once to the kitchen staircase. The old lady had given me the latch-key with such a free hand that I felt myself fully justified in walking in; in fact, I rather wanted to take her by surprise if possible.

Nevertheless I made a little noise going downstairs to give her knowledge of my approach, and it was then that I thought I heard a window open somewhere at the back of the house.

I walked towards the end of the passage, and there I saw the glow of the fire reflected through the open door of the handsome sitting-room in which I had sat with the old lady on the previous day. It played upon the opposite wall as I advanced with a great air of comfort.

"Ten to one," I said to myself, "that I find the old lady asleep over the fire."

The room I found in darkness except for the firelight. I could see little within it. I paused on the threshold and made a polite inquiry.

"May I come in?" I asked in a tone intended to be loud enough to wake the old lady.

No answer.

I advanced into the room with my candle and

set it on the table, then I struck a match and lit two more of the candles in the sconces.

The room was empty!

This placed me rather in a dilemma. I had no further means of announcing my presence; I could only wait.

I sat down by the fire and began to look around.

Comfortable, even luxurious as the room was with its abundance of valuable knick-knacks and pictures, it had an eerie look about it. The eyes of the figures in the pictures seemed following me about.

I got up and lit two more of the candles in the sconces on the walls. Then I returned to my seat, made up the fire, and waited the course of events.

I waited thus quite a quarter of an hour, during which nothing occurred, and then I heard sounds which almost made me jump from my chair.

The first was a long, gasping breath, followed after an interval by a groan, a long wailing groan as of one in the deepest suffering.

I immediately rose from my chair, and caught a glimpse of my white face as I did so in the looking-glass over the mantelpiece.

I stood for some seconds on the hearthrug, and then the groan was repeated; it came from the direction of a heavy curtain which hung in one corner of the room, and which I had taken, on the previous day, to be the covering of a cabinet or a recess in the wall perhaps for some of the old lady's out-door clothing.

I tore it on one side now and found that it concealed a door. The knob turned in my hand and I entered the room beyond; it was in total darkness, and I at once returned to the sitting-room for candles.

I took two in my hands and advanced once again, with an effort, into the dark room.

The sight that met my gaze there almost caused me to drop them. It was a handsomely furnished bedroom, and in the farther corner was the bed. On it lay the old lady wrapped in a white quilted silk dressing-robe.

The whole of the breast of this garment was saturated with blood!

With the candles trembling in my hands I advanced to the side of the bed, and the poor soul's eyes looked up at me while she acknowledged my coming with a groan.

Looking down at her there could not be a doubt but that her throat had been cut!

I drew back from her horrified, and then I saw her lips moving; she was trying to speak.

I put my ear down close to her mouth and then I heard faintly but very distinctly two words –

"Safe – open."

I answered her at once.

"I will go for a doctor first, then I will return

and open the safe."

At once she moved her head, causing a fresh flow of blood from a great gaping wound at the right side of her neck. She was eager to speak again, and I bent my ear over her mouth.

Two words came again very faintly – "Open – first."

I nodded to show her that I understood what she meant, then giving one glance at her I prepared to do what she asked. There was a look of satisfaction in her eyes as I turned away. I went quickly back into the sitting-room and turned the carved rose on the left side of the frame of the looking-glass in the over-mantel. Then when the glass had slid up I felt for the spring in the wall, touched it, and the door flew open. Without any hesitation I fixed the key in the lock of the steel safe, and, with a slight effort, turned it and pulled the door open.

The first thing I saw was a slip of white paper with some writing on it lying on two packets. This I took up and read at once; the words scribbled on it were in a lady's hand.

"If anything has happened to me take these two packets, hide them in your pockets, and close the safe, cupboard, and looking-glass, and leave it all as it was at first."

I did not delay a moment. I took the two packets, which were wrapped in white paper like chemists' parcels, and sealed with red wax. I saw this before I crammed them into my trousers pockets.

I hastily closed the safe, locked it, fastened the panel, and, by turning the rose on the right-hand side of the over-mantel, caused the glass to resume its place.

Then I turned to leave the room, and – found myself standing face to face with Saumarez, the man with the glass eye, who held a revolver levelled at me.

He did not stay to speak, but fired immediately; I dodged my head to one side just in time and heard the bullet go crashing into the looking-glass behind me.

Before he could fire again I hit him with all my might under the ear, and he fell in the corner of the room like a log. Stopping only to possess myself of his revolver, which had dropped by his side, I rushed up the stairs and out into the street; there I inquired of the first person I met, a working man going home, for the nearest doctor, and he directed me to a Dr. Redfern only about ten doors away.

Within a few seconds I was pausing at this door, and endeavouring to make an astonished parlour-maid understand that I wanted to see her master on a matter of life and death.

A placid-looking gentleman made his appearance from a room at the end of the entrance hall while I was speaking to her, with an evening paper in his hand.

"What's the matter?" he asked casually.

"Murder is the matter," I answered between

gasps of excitement, "murder at Number 190, and I want you to come at once."

I gave him a brief account of the old lady with her throat cut. He stood looking at me a moment or two, as if in doubt whether I was sane or not, then made up his mind.

"All right," he said, "just wait a moment and I'll come with you."

He reappeared in about a couple of minutes, wearing an overcoat and a tall hat.

"Now," he said, "just lead the way."

We went together straight back to Number 190, and I think he had some misgivings about entering the house with me alone, but I reassured him by reminding him that an old lady was dying within; as it was he made me go first.

"I had no idea any one lived here at all," he remarked, as I lighted him along the passage to the stairs by means of wax vestas, of which I fortunately had a supply, for there was no candle in the hall. "I always thought this house was shut up. But still I have only been here just over twelve months."

"I think you will find," I said, as we got firmly on the basement floor, and saw the reflection of my candle which I had left on the table in the sitting-room, "that there are a good many surprises in this house."

"Now," I continued as we entered the room, "the old lady is lying in there. I will take this candle and show you the way." I led the way into the room, and held the candle aloft, with a shudder at what I expected to see there.

The bed was empty.

I rubbed my eyes and looked again.

No, there was nothing there; the bed looked rather rumpled, but there was no sign whatever of the old lady.

"Well," remarked the doctor sharply – he had followed closely at my heels – "where is your murdered old lady?"

I looked round the bedroom helplessly.

"I would take the most solemn oath," I said steadfastly, "that I left the old lady lying on that bed with her throat cut, and her clothes and the bed appeared soaked in blood."

The doctor walked to the bed and examined it closely, turning back the bedclothes.

"There is not a spot of blood on it," he remarked savagely, "you are dreaming."

But my eyes were sharper than his.

"Look here," I said, and pointed to a small red mark on the wall on the farther side of the bed, "what do you call that?" He leaned over the bed and looked at the little stain through his glasses as I held the light.

"Yes," he said after a close scrutiny, "that *might* be blood, and, strange to say, it seems wet."

He looked at his finger which had just touched

it, and it had a slight smear of blood on it.

I had told him on the staircase that I had been attacked by a man who had fired at me, and indeed the smell of powder even on the landing above was very apparent.

"Now come back into the next room," I said, "and see the body of the man who assailed me and whom I knocked down."

He followed me into the boudoir, and I went straight to the corner where I had last seen Saumarez lying.

There was nothing there!

I gave a great gasp of astonishment.

"I left the man lying there!" I exclaimed, pointing to the floor.

The doctor took the candle lamp from my hands and held it close to my face, scrutinising me earnestly meanwhile through his glasses; then he leant forward and sniffed suspiciously.

"Do you drink?" he asked abruptly.

Then, noticing my look of growing indignation, he altered his tone slightly.

"Excuse my asking the question," he explained. "But it is the only way in which I can account for your symptoms. Do you see things?"

"Things be d – – ," I replied hotly. "I would answer with my life that I left that poor old lady lying on her bed grievously wounded not half an hour

31

ago, and the villain who assaulted me insensible in this corner!"

The doctor went to the corner and held the candle in such a way as to shed its light upon the floor.

Then he stooped and picked up something.

"What's this?" he exclaimed, holding it close to the candle. "A glass eye," he continued in astonishment, "a glass eye, as I live!"

"There!" I said triumphantly, "the man who fired at me had a glass eye. Is it not a brown one, shot with blood?"

"Right!" he answered after another glance at it, "a bloodshot brown eye it undoubtedly is."

He handed it to me, and I put it in my pocket.

"You had better take care of it," he said. "But I really don't know what to say about your story."

"Perhaps you will deny the evidence of your eyes?" I asked; "look at this."

I pointed to where the bullet from the revolver had struck the looking-glass over the mantelpiece and starred it.

"No," he answered, "that certainly looks as if it had been smashed by a bullet. There is the little round hole where the bullet entered. And there is another point too," he continued, "you say you left the old lady lying on the bed bleeding, not half an hour ago?"

"Certainly."

"Then the bed ought to be warm; let us come and see."

We walked back into the bedroom and examined the bed again.

It was very evident to me that a fresh coverlet had been put on the bed and fresh sheets. How it could have been done in so short a time was a marvel to me.

The doctor put his hand on the coverlet.

"That is quite cold," he reported, "there can be no question of a doubt about that."

"Let me try inside the bed," I suggested; "that may tell a different tale."

I turned down the bedclothes, and put my hand into the bed. It was distinctly warm!

"Now," I said, turning to the doctor, "do you believe me or not?"

He put his hand into the bed.

"Yes," he answered, "it is certainly warm. I don't know what to make of it."

I thrust my hand once more deep beneath the clothes, and this time it encountered something and closed on it. I glanced at it as I drew it out.

It was a lady's handkerchief.

I don't know what moved me to do it, but an impulse made me put it in my pocket, without showing it to the doctor.

"I don't know what to make of it at all," repeated Dr. Redfern, stroking his chin, "but one thing is certain, we must acquaint the police."

"Certainly," I answered. "I think we ought to have done that long ago."

"Well, will you promise me to remain here, Mr. – Mr. – ?" he queried.

"Anstruther," I suggested. People in the middle class of life always assume that you are a "Mr." I might have been a Duke!

"Will you promise me to remain here, Mr. Anstruther," he asked, "while I go and telephone the police?"

"Of course," I answered; "what should I want to run away for?"

"Very well, then," he said with a nod and a smile. "I will take it that you won't. I will be back inside a quarter of an hour."

We lit more of the candles on the walls, and then I took the candle lamp to light him upstairs to the front door.

I was standing there watching him going up Monmouth Street towards his house, when a sudden resolve took possession of me concerning the two packets I had in my trousers pockets! I did not know what turn affairs were going to take, and I thought I should like to put those two little parcels in a place of safety.

I had noticed a small dismal post office at the

end of the street not fifty yards off. I would go and post them, registered to my lawyers, in whom I had the greatest confidence.

To the taking of this resolve and the carrying of it out, instead of returning to the downstairs room, I always attribute, in the light of subsequent events, the saving of my life. I left the door "on the jar" and ran quickly to the post office. There I demanded their largest sized registered envelope, and they fortunately had a big one.

Into this I crammed the two packets – which I noticed were both directed to me in a very neat lady's hand – and then, as an afterthought, the handkerchief which I had found in the bed. Finally I put the key of the safe in too. With my back to the ever curious clerk, I directed it to myself –

c/o Messrs. BLACKETT & SNOWDON, Solicitors, Lincoln's Inn, London.

Then, slapping it down before the astonished official, I demanded a receipt for it.

This obtained, I hastened back to 190; the door was still as I had left it, but in a few moments the doctor returned, and at his heels a policeman.

"The inspector will be here directly," announced Dr. Redfern. "We had better wait outside until he arrives."

We walked up and down for nearly a quarter of an hour while the doctor smoked a cigarette, and meanwhile the policeman, a person of gigantic stature and a bucolic expression of countenance, eyed me suspiciously.

Presently the inspector arrived, and the doctor and I returned with him to the sitting-room downstairs. There the police official insisted upon my giving a full account of the whole matter, while he stood critically by with a notebook in his hand. I told him the whole truth from the time of my seeing the old lady at the door, to the time of my calling in the doctor, but I suppressed all mention of the two packets and the secret safe. These being confidential matters between me and the old lady, I did not feel at liberty to disclose them.

I saw very plainly from the looks the inspector gave me that he did not believe me; he even had doubts, it was very evident, whether I was staying at the Hotel Magnifique at all, as I had informed him at the commencement of my statement.

Having entered all the notes to his satisfaction, he thoroughly inspected both rooms and made more notes. Then he went outside and bawled up the stairs –

"Wilkins!"

"Sir," came the answer from the bucolic constable on duty above.

"Just step round to the 'Compasses,'" instructed his superior from the foot of the stairs, "and tell my brother I should be glad if he'd come round here for a few minutes. We've got a rather curious case."

"Very good, sir," came the reply, followed by the heavy tread of the man's boots as he went to carry out the orders.

"My brother's down 'ere on a bit of a 'oliday, sir," explained the inspector to the doctor, entirely ignoring me, "and being one of the tip-top detectives up in London, I thought we'd take the benefit of his opinion."

The "Compasses," as it turned out, being only a couple of streets off, we had not long to wait for the coming of the detective luminary from London. His heavy footsteps were soon heard on the stairs; preceded by the constable, he descended the flight with evident forethought and consideration. Emerging from the darkness into the light of the wax candles, he presented the appearance of a prosperous butcher, tall, broad-shouldered, red-necked, and with moustache and whiskers of a sandy hue. His face was very red, and the skin shining as if distended with good living.

"This is my brother, Inspector Bull of the Z Metropolitan Division," explained our inspector to the doctor, once more ignoring me, "down 'ere on a little 'oliday."

As I learned afterwards, this gentleman was one of the Guardian Angels who watched over the safety of the inhabitants of the Mile End Road.

The doctor having shaken hands with him, his brother put another question to him.

"'Ow's Alf?" he inquired.

The newcomer gently soothed the back of his red neck with a hand like a small leg of mutton, and displayed a set of massive front teeth in a gratified smile.

"'E's all right," he answered, "we wos having fifty up when you sent for me."

"You see," explained our inspector, "my brother's got so many friends in the licensed victuallers' line down here, through being a Mason, that it takes him 'arf his 'oliday to go round and see 'em all."

The doctor smiled indulgently but made no answer; then our inspector briefly informed his brother of the state of the case before him, stating the facts as I related them, in such a different light, and with so many evident aspersions on my veracity, that I hardly knew them again.

The two brothers made a further close inspection of the rooms, and then held a consultation on the hearthrug in whispers.

Though the words were unintelligible, the fact that the officer of the Z Division had been partaking liberally of whisky soon became apparent from the all-pervading odour of that stimulant diffused throughout the apartment.

They finished at last, and I heard the London man's final word of advice –

"I should put me 'and on 'im at any rate."

Chapter IV. I am Detained

I was the "'im" referred to evidently.

Our inspector buttoned up his blue overcoat.

"Perhaps you'll be kind enough to walk down with us to the station, Mr. ... er – Anstruther," he said; "we can have a little talk down there and straighten things out a bit."

His subterfuge did not in the least deceive me.

"Do I understand," I asked, "that you propose to detain me?"

The inspector raised his shoulders perplexedly, and his brother smiled a fat smile over his shoulder.

"That'll depend how you explain matters to our chief," he said deprecatingly; "at any rate we'd better get along."

This was a hint I could not disregard. He led the way up the staircase, and his stout brother, through force of habit, closed in behind, far too close to be pleasant, owing to the diffused aroma of a mixture of various brands of inferior whisky, arising from his hard breathing as he ascended the stairs. We walked two and two down Monmouth Street, I with the inspector, the doctor and the London detective improving their acquaintance in the rear.

Two streets off we dropped the officer of the Z Division, who betook himself once more to the "Compasses" to continue his "fifty up" with his friend the landlord, and the doctor joined us. I had the pleasure of listening to his conversation with the inspector, conducted across me, without having the pleasure of being included in it.

We walked all three down into the town, and then straight into the Police Station, only a few doors off my hotel.

The inspector and the doctor went into a private room to confer with some superior official while I was left to sit by the fire in the outer office.

Presently the inspector came out.

"We've decided to detain you, Mr. Anstruther," he said, "until we can find out a little more about this affair. Just come over here."

"Look here, Mr. Inspector," I said, "if you intend to detain me without sufficient reason, you'll find it an awkward matter." The inspector looked a trifle uncomfortable.

"We shall have to take our chance of that," he said, rather sullenly, "we've only got our duty to do, Mr. Anstruther. You can have bail, I should think."

"Bail!" I repeated, "how am I to get bail? I don't know a soul in the town."

The inspector shrugged his shoulders and motioned me into a railed space in the centre of the office.

There was no help for it, so I went and placed myself as he desired in the little dock, and a constable standing there obligingly clamped down a rail behind me to keep me there. Then the doctor, who, it turned out, was some official in the town, gave a garbled version of the whole affair, which I found it useless to try and contradict, as I was told to hold my tongue. The inspector's version of the affair was even more insulting than the doctor's. He did not hesitate to express his opinion that I was a very suspicious person, probably a lunatic at large. When asked if I had anything to say, my remark summed up the situation, tersely, in a few words.

"This is a parcel of d – d rot!" I said.

Then they searched me.

The inspector simply gloated over Saumarez' revolver when I turned it out of my pocket, and this feeling rose to an absolute thrill of triumph when he discovered that one of the chambers had been discharged.

In my heart, I was thankful that I had sent those two packets and the key to my lawyers.

While the inspector was hanging fondly over Saumarez' glass eye, which one energetic young constable had furraged out of the corner of my waistcoat pocket, an idea struck me which ought to have occurred to me before.

I had come to Bath with a letter of introduction to a certain doctor, a Dr. Mainwaring; I would send for him.

"Look here, Mr. Inspector," I said, "when you've quite finished rattling me about, I have two suggestions to make. One is to send some of your men to try if they can find the old lady whose throat has been cut, and the other is to send for Dr. Mainwaring, who knows me. I warn you that if you lock me up you will get into trouble."

At the mention of Dr. Mainwaring, Dr. Redfern, who was still there, pricked up his ears.

"Dr. Mainwaring!" he repeated. "Do you know him?"

"I came here about ten days ago," I answered, "with a letter of introduction to him from Sir Belgrave Walpole. I've no doubt that he will be able to tell you something about me."

He turned to the inspector.

"Don't you think you had better send a man up to Royal Crescent," he said, "to ask Dr. Mainwaring? There *may* be a mistake, you know. It would be safer."

I could see that the inspector was very unwilling to admit the possibility of a mistake; he was, however, overruled by the man who was writing in the book, and who appeared to be a person in authority.

"Shapland," he said to a waiting constable, "go up to Dr. Mainwaring's and ask if he knows a person of the name of Anstruther."

"You'd better take one of my cards there with you," I suggested, "then he'll know who you mean."

The inspector gave me a scathing look, but gave the man one of the cards out of my case.

I think they were undecided then as to whether they would lock me up or not, but eventually made up their minds on the side of prudence.

I was allowed to sit by the fire.

Within half an hour a motor came puffing up to the police station, and Dr. Mainwaring entered.

"My dear Mr. Anstruther," he inquired breathlessly, "whatever is the matter?"

In a few brief sentences I unloaded the burden of my wrongs.

"Why, there must be some mistake!" cried Mainwaring. "I'll just go off and see the chief constable, he's a particular friend of mine."

When he had gone, the faces of my guardians grew visibly longer; one of them fetched me an armchair out of the office.

The chief constable soon put matters right.

"This gentleman is staying at the Magnifique," he announced, "he is well known to Dr. Mainwaring, and, in fact, the doctor will answer for his appearance; what more do you want, Mr. Inspector?"

The inspector wanted nothing more.

Within five minutes I was sitting by a glorious fire in a private room at the Magnifique, discussing the whole matter with the chief constable and Dr. Mainwaring.

But before I left the station, I put a query to Inspector Bull, junior.

"What have you done about the old lady?" I asked.

The officer assumed some shreds of dignity, even in his discomfiture.

"You may have thought us a bit forgetful, sir," he observed, "but I assure you, both the railway stations have been under careful observation from the time of my being able to touch a telephone."

"Thank you," I said; but it appeared to me that under the circumstances they might just as profitably have watched the Pump Room or the Baths.

Chapter V. Arrested

Being left to myself after thoroughly thrashing out the whole case with Dr. Mainwaring and the chief constable, who both agreed with me that the circumstances were the most extraordinary they had ever heard of, I sat down to consider matters by myself.

Here was I, a country gentleman of moderate estate, trying to eke out a smallish income by literature, plumped down into the centre of as fine a tangle of mystery as ever came out of the *Arabian Nights Entertainments*.

I got up and looked at myself in the glass, and saw there a clean-shaven tall man of thirty whose black hair was already turning white at the temples; about my grey eyes, alas, there were already crows' feet, the price I had paid, I suppose, for taking honours at Oxford.

I sat down again and thought deeply.

"Bill Anstruther," I said to myself, "you're in for it. You've consented to receive the confidences of that old lady, who, poor soul, was in the direst need of help and friendship without doubt when she called you in the night before last. You're bound in honour to go through with it, and try to help her, or at any rate carry out her wishes, be she dead or alive."

Thus I reasoned, and in this, it seemed to me, my duty lay. Obviously the first thing to do was to obtain possession of the packets again and ascertain their contents. I knew, of course, that they were directed to me and possibly contained some request of the old lady. I marvelled very much what the connection between her and the man with the glass eye could possibly be, but could form no guess even in the matter. It was very evident that he was a blood-thirsty scoundrel, and I had little doubt in my own mind that it was he who had wounded her, perhaps unto death.

While I thought of it, I decided to go down to the office and make inquiries concerning Saumarez.

I found he had left during the morning.

"Mr. Saumarez went up to town, sir," explained the clerk, "by the twelve-twenty."

"Thank you," I said, and walked away to the smoking-room to have a good think again. Eating for the present was out of the question.

After three cigarettes I arrived at the following conclusions. I would go up to town in the morning, secure the packets, and read them in my lawyers' office.

I would not trust myself to carry them about with me while that man Saumarez was at large. It was very evident that the safe and its contents possessed a great attraction for him; probably with very good reason.

I caught the morning train to London, and arrived in Lincoln's Inn about two o'clock, after lunching early at my club. There Messrs. Blackett & Snowdon's managing clerk handed me the registered packet which I had sent off the evening before from the post office in Monmouth Street, Bath.

With this in my hand I retired to the private office of Mr. Snowdon, who was away from town, his room being placed at my disposal by the managing clerk when I told him I had some important papers to examine.

I sat down at the desk, cleared it of the few papers lying there, then prepared to open my precious parcel.

First I tore off the registered envelope.

Yes, there were the two packets which I had thought so much of in the hours I lay awake during the night. There was the key; there was the handkerchief.

I took this latter up and examined it carefully by the light. It was of the finest cambric, and bore in the corner the letter C.

Then there remained the two packets to examine.

They were both addressed to me in a small, old-fashioned handwriting which I took to be that of the old lady, poor soul! One was heavy, felt hard, and contained evidently a box of some sort, the other was soft and I took it to be composed of papers. I broke the seals – a C – and opened it. My surmise was correct, it contained several sheets of thick correspondence paper, covered with writing. It was dated the day I first met her. When I spread it out this is what I found it to contain –

"DEAR MR. ANSTRUTHER, – I have little doubt but you consider me merely a crazy old woman.

"Perhaps I am, Heaven knows I have had enough trouble in my life to make me so, and the trouble and anxiety I am enduring now is by no means the lightest I have had to bear. That is why I had the resolve to trust you, taking a sudden fancy, as I have done before without regretting it, to a resolute open face.

"I believe that you will carry out what I ask of you to the letter; I believe you will do it honestly and truly, for the reason that you love to be honest and true.

"So much for my trust in you. Now for the object of my appealing to you.

"I am threatened with a great peril, a peril which may cost me my life, I expect it, I do not fear it. I have held my life in my hands for years past.

"But there is something in my case which I value more than my life; this I would preserve at all costs. It is contained in the small box in the second packet which I have prepared for you.

"I think I have thought of every contingency and may reasonably count upon being left in peace until I see you at five to-morrow. I do not doubt for one moment but that you will keep your appointment. Should I, however, have to send you to the safe, instead of handing you these packets, I have prepared even for that.

"The request I am about to make you is, I know, an unreasonable one, yet I believe you will carry it out.

"Upon opening the other packet, which I shall leave you with this, you will find a small carved casket which is locked; with it you will find sufficient money for your journey – of which presently.

"Mr. Anstruther, I want you to take the casket to Aquazilia and to deliver it to the person to whom it is addressed."

"Aquazilia!" I exclaimed, putting down the letter, "why, that is the big Republic the other side of Brazil which once upon a time used to be a Monarchy! That's rather a tall order!" I took the letter up again and went on: –

"I know the journey is a long one, but it will repay you. When you told me you were a writer, I knew at once that such a journey would be one from which you would draw profit both in experience and otherwise. In doing it you will earn my undying gratitude. Go, I beseech you! To you I confide that which is dearer to me than my life. Go, I implore of you. I ask it in the name of Truth and Honour. Go, and earn the eternal thanks of

"CARLOTTA D'ALTENBERG."

"D'Altenberg, d'Altenberg," I muttered as I finished. "It seems a familiar name!"

I now turned my attention to the second packet, and opened that. It contained a small wooden box with the lid tied down with string. Upon taking this off, I found within a very beautifully carved oblong casket, made of ebony, inlaid with gold. It was a most finished piece of workmanship, and measured, I should think, about six inches by perhaps two and a half. In raised letters on the lid was carved the letter C as on the seals. On a small parchment label firmly secured to it by silk was: –

"To His Excellency the Senor JUAN D'ALTA, Valoro, Aquazilia."

It was fastened by no less than three locks, all of different sizes, and by its excessive weight, even for ebony, I should say was lined with some metal.

When I had lifted this casket out of the box I found beneath it two ordinary long envelopes both addressed to me and open. On the first I took up was: –

"To William Anstruther, Esq. For the expenses of the journey to Valoro."

I opened it and found it to contain four fifty pound notes. On the other was my name, and beneath it: –

"A slight honorarium by way of compensation for time lost on the journey."

It contained a Bank of England note for one thousand pounds. I sat with the note in my hand for some time; it was the first for that amount which I had ever come across.

However, not without some considerable satisfaction, I admit, I put up the note into its envelope again and packed it with the other into the box. I very carefully replaced the ebony casket after a glance of admiration at its beautifully inlaid workmanship.

I closed the box up as before, and, making free with Mr. Snowdon's stationery, put it in a fresh linen lined envelope and sealed it up again. This time with my own seal. I treated the letter in the same way, packing it up with the hankerchief and the key, then directed the two to myself, care of my lawyers. I intended to leave both in their care as before. I had ample confidence in their strong room. I had barely completed this task and thrown the old wrappers into the fire, when there came a knock at the door; the managing clerk entered with rather a scared look on his face.

"There are two men waiting to see you downstairs, Mr. Anstruther," he announced, "and I rather think they are police officers."

Instinctively as he spoke I thrust the two packets before me into pigeon holes of the writing table I was sitting at, and he saw me do it.

Before I could make any reply, the door was pushed open behind him, and two men entered; the foremost of them walked up to the table.

"Are you Mr. William Anstruther?" he asked.

He was a tall, dark, fresh-coloured man with sharp grey eyes, his companion had the appearance of an ordinary constable in plain clothes.

"Yes," I answered, rising, "I am William Anstruther."

"Then I arrest you, William Anstruther," he said, "on suspicion of causing the death of an old lady, name unknown, whose body was discovered at daybreak this morning on Lansdown, near Bath, with her throat cut. You'll have to come with us down to Bath to be charged."

Here was a terrible development!

My first thoughts were of pity for the poor old lady. How I wished I had been able to save her life.

"Very well," I answered as coolly as I could. "I suppose there is no help for it, and I had better go with you. Perhaps, Mr. Watson," I said, turning to the managing clerk, who was standing by as white as a sheet, "perhaps you will see that this man has proper authority for taking me."

"Certainly, Mr. Anstruther," he answered, then turning to the detective he asked for his papers.

"Show me your warrant, please," he said. "I shall not allow Mr. Anstruther, our client, to leave with you unless you do."

The fresh-coloured officer smiled, and produced from his pocket a blue paper, together with some other documents. These seemed to satisfy Watson.

"There seems no help for it, Mr. Anstruther," he said, with them in his hands. "I am afraid you will have to go with him. This is a proper warrant signed by a magistrate on sworn information."

"Who are the informants?" I asked.

He referred to the warrant and read out the names.

"Inspector James Bull, Frederick Redfern, surgeon, and Anthony Saumarez, gentleman."

"Saumarez!" I exclaimed, "the scoundrel and would-be murderer!"

"You had better be careful what you say," remarked the police officer, "as I may have to take it down, and it will be used against you."

"Yes," confirmed Watson, "you'd better say as little as possible. No doubt the whole matter is a mistake."

I took up my overcoat and the managing clerk helped me on with it; meanwhile, the police officer walked to the desk I had been sitting at and laid his hands on some papers. I looked upon the packets as lost.

Watson, however, stopped him at once.

"You mustn't touch those papers," he said hastily. "They are the property of Mr. Snowdon, a member of our firm."

"Then what is *he* doing here?" asked the man, with a jerk of his head towards me.

"Mr. Anstruther," replied Watson, "was attending to some business correspondence at Mr. Snowdon's desk, that gentleman being away."

"Where's the correspondence?" asked the detective, with a quick glance at my two packets sticking out of the pigeon holes. I looked the man straight in the face.

"My correspondence is finished," I answered, "and in the hands of this firm."

A little smile about Watson's mouth and a hasty glance at the packets, convinced me that he understood my remark.

"Very well, then," said the police officer, "we'd better come along. Provided you come quietly," he observed to me as I followed him out, "it won't be necessary for me to handcuff you."

That was a comfort I thought, as I went downstairs and through the office, full of astounded clerks, who had all known me well for years.

We got into a cab and were driven to Paddington Station, reaching it about dusk, much to my satisfaction, as I should not at all have appreciated making my appearance in such a place with the two police officers.

We got into a third class compartment all to ourselves right at the end of the train, near the engine, and there I sat between the two men, who hardly exchanged a word the whole way, but who sat trying to read newspapers by the bad light. They would hold no conversation with me.

When we got to Bath they hurried me quickly down the stairs into a fly, and then we drove straight through the town.

As we passed the police station and my hotel – towards which I cast longing glances, for it was not far off dinner time – I asked a question of the tall, fresh-coloured man.

"I understood that you were going to take me to the police station?" I said.

The man shook his head.

"We are taking you to the prison," he said, "for the night. You will be brought before the magistrates in the morning."

I sank back in the corner of the fly thoroughly dejected, and the vehicle drove out by what I knew to be the Warminster Road. We now left the lights of the town behind, and then the journey was entirely between two hedgerows, which bordered the road, with an occasional field gate by way of variety – all else beyond was blank night, for there was no moon.

My two guardians began to show signs of fatigue, not unmixed with a certain disgust, at the length of the journey.

They began yawning and stretching their arms, with very little regard for my comfort.

When at last the fly pulled up with a jerk, after a good deal of bumping over a rough road, the two men were very unceremonious in ordering me to quit the vehicle.

"Now then, Ugly," remarked the fresh-coloured man with a push of his foot, which was remarkably like a kick, "out you get!"

He stepped out himself and I followed, knowing full well it was useless to resist, but I made a mental resolve that I would report him.

Once outside the fly, I found myself apparently at the foot of a tower, a door stood open in front of me, and on the doorstep a man holding a lantern.

I was, however, given very little time to contemplate this scene; the big man seized my right arm, and his companion my left; between them, they rushed me up a flight of steps immediately inside the tower.

These steps constituted a spiral staircase which wound round the interior of the tower; ever and anon as we passed a small window I saw the lights of Bath twinkling in the distance.

Beyond a few walks during the ten days I had spent there – my first visit – I knew very little of Bath or its neighbourhood, therefore I had no opportunity of taking my bearings.

I was urged up this staircase in a manner which I should have thought unusual had I not remembered the men's complaints of the long journey – which they had made twice – in the fly.

Finally we reached a door, and they simply pushed me through it into a large room. It was evidently the top storey of the tower and had windows looking all ways. It was perfectly circular in shape, was fairly clean, and had a fire burning in a grate with a wire screen before it; in one corner was a bed.

The two men released their hold as I looked around, and the dark one went to a corner and picked up a chain.

"Come here!" he shouted to me roughly.

His colleague assisted me by giving me a shove in his direction. Then, in a twinkling, he fixed a steel ring to my left ankle, snapped it there and locked a small padlock on it.

I was chained up like a dog!

Having thoroughly searched me, they prepared to leave; the taller man addressed me.

"I suppose you know," he remarked, as the two moved towards the door, "that if you make any attempt to escape, you'll be shot?"

With this parting caution he closed the door, and I heard a key turn in the lock.

I took one turn round the room, the chain being long enough, with many a yearning look at the distant lights of Bath; then, horrified at the clanking of my fetters, which were fixed to a staple in the wall, I threw myself as I was on the bed in the corner, and there, being tired out, almost immediately fell asleep.

Chapter VI. Put to the Torture

I awoke with a feeling of intense cold, the fire was out, and I was lying outside the bed without covering.

The day had fully broken, and there was even an attempt on the part of the sun to pierce the heavy mists of a November morning. I looked around out of the windows, and saw the hills topped with cloud in every direction.

Drawing the rough blankets over me, I lay and thought. My first yearning was for something to eat; I had tasted nothing since lunch the previous day; I was fearfully hungry.

I had lain thus perhaps half an hour between sleeping and waking, when a key was put in the door and it opened, admitting a big, dark man with a long, black beard; he bore in his hands a small table which he placed in the middle of the room.

"Now," I said to myself, "this means breakfast."

I was mistaken.

He brought in next a square box, not unlike the case of a sewing machine, and placed it on the table.

"What can this be?" I muttered as I watched him closely.

In a few minutes footsteps were heard on the stairs, and another man joined him. A great strong fellow with a fair moustache. The two of them wheeled a large chair with glass arms to it, which I had not noticed before, from one corner of the room, and placed it on one side of the table.

The preparations now had all the appearance of the commencement of some performance; it only needed the principal actor to appear.

He was not long in coming.

Meanwhile, I wondered why the chair had glass arms to it.

I noticed that the two men, who now stood idly looking out of the windows, did not wear uniforms. They were dressed in ordinary rough-looking clothes of foreign cut; it struck me as very strange. I asked them who they were.

"Are you the warders of the prison?" I said.

"Hein!" the dark one inquired.

"Are you the warders of the prison?" I repeated.

"Find out, *verdammt Englander*," the man replied.

Then I felt certain I was in no English prison. Where was I?

The question was soon answered, the door once more opened and *Saumarez* entered. I sat up on the bed and fairly gasped; the whole matter was perfectly unintelligible to me. After the first thrill of astonishment my glance went to his eyes.

They were complete; he had another glass one in the socket, and it exactly matched the real one.

He came towards me with a little bow, and a smile on his red countenance.

"Good morning, Mr. Anstruther," he began, "we seem to be always meeting."

I could not restrain my feelings.

"That is my misfortune," I answered.

He smiled and shrugged his shoulders.

"Perhaps so," he answered casually, "that remains to be seen."

He said some words in German to the two men, which I imperfectly understood, but it seemed to be an order to lift me off the bed, for they immediately did it.

Then one of them unlocked my chain, and the two of them carried me to the chair, and sat me in it.

I now realised that I was in a desperate condition.

"I insist on knowing," I cried to Saumarez, "why I was brought here. It is very evident that I have been tricked."

Saumarez laughed – a low laugh of enjoyment.

"You certainly came here under a false impression," he sniggered; "as for the reason of your coming, you will soon know it. Now, to begin with, where is the key of the safe at 190 Monmouth Street. You have been thoroughly searched and we cannot find it."

"You are not likely to," I answered. "It is in a place where you cannot get at it."

"Indeed!" replied Saumarez. "What place is

that?"

"I shall not tell you."

"We shall see," he remarked laconically.

As he spoke, he motioned to the two men to do something with the box on the table.

As they moved towards it, I heard the double report of a sporting gun not far off. Evidently some one was out shooting.

The men went to the table, and, taking off the square lid of the box, disclosed a large galvanic battery!

My blood began to run cold as an awful idea formed itself in my mind.

"Secure him in the chair!" Saumarez said sharply in German.

Before the men could reach me, I darted out of the chair towards the door, but they were too quick for me and caught me before I reached it. They carried me back struggling to the chair, and one held me down in it while the other passed thick straps round me, holding me fast in it, hand and foot. I found, when they had done with me, that my two hands were strapped firmly to the glass arms of the chair.

Lying back in the chair I noticed high up in the roof an old cobwebbed window, the top of which was standing open for purposes of ventilation. It looked as if it had not been interfered with for years.

In the position I was in, I could not very well

see what was going on in the room, but the next thing I experienced was feeling my wrists being encircled apparently with wire. I gave one convulsive struggle to get free, but it was useless I knew well now what they were going to do.

They were going to torture me by giving me galvanic shocks, and passing strong currents through my body.

I had heard of the torture being applied in Russia to political prisoners.

I had, when a boy, patronised those machines which professed to try one's "nerve." I had held the two handles and watched the proprietor draw out the rod from the coil to increase the strength of the current. I knew how unbearable *that* feeling could become even with a *weak* battery. What would it be with this *strong* one?

Saumarez' voice broke in upon me.

"Where is the key of the safe?"

I was enraged at the sound of his voice.

"You shall never know, you vile devil!" I cried.

"Give it to him," he exclaimed sharply to the two men in German. As he spoke I heard the sharp report of two sporting guns, one charged with black powder, one, from its quick sharp crack, with smokeless, *quite near*. There were two sportsmen.

Then – oh my God! – began that awful torture of a strong current of electricity passing up my arms.

I threw back my head and cried with all my

strength, directing my voice to the open window far above me in the roof of the tower –

"Help! Murder! Help!"

And immediately, to my great joy, I heard an answering shout!

"*Donner und blitzen*!" cried Saumarez, "he has attracted their attention! Stop his mouth!"

Immediately I felt a handkerchief being rammed into my mouth, but from far below came the sound of hard knocking on the door of the tower, and men's voices shouting.

Saumarez rapped out a fearful oath, and gave an order to the men.

"You must carry him down below and drop him through the trap door into the vaults," he cried. "You will have plenty of time to do it if you are quick. Unbind him, sharp now!"

The two men commenced to do as he told them and very soon had the straps off me, then they carried me between them towards the door after firmly securing the gag in my mouth.

They had got about half-way down the spiral staircase with me, Saumarez following behind, and I was in an agony of mind that they would succeed in reaching the vaults with me, when I heard the door burst in below, and a cheer from several voices, followed by rapid footsteps on the steps.

"It's no good," cried Saumarez with another oath, "drop him and follow me up to the roof."

They did drop me very roughly on the stone stairs, but before they went I heard one of the men cry out –

"Don't kill him in cold blood!"

Then there came the click of a pistol lock followed by a deafening report, and a bullet struck the step I was lying on about an inch from my temple. There was a scuffling of feet on the stairs above, mingled with words of remonstrance in German; the two men were hurrying Saumarez away.

The report and the impact of the bullet had half stunned me, but I sat up, and my hands being free, tore the gag out of my mouth. At the same time, rapid footsteps came up the stairs, and, in a few moments, I found a very familiar face, with an absolutely astounded expression on it looking down into mine.

"In Heaven's name!" a well-known voice cried, "what are you doing here, Bill?"

It was my cousin, Lord St. Nivel, a subaltern in the Coldstream Guards!

Chapter VII. Cruft's Folly

Looking over my cousin's shoulders were two other faces, one covered with rough hair, and evidently belonging to a game-keeper, the other the beautiful face of my cousin, Lady Ethel Vanborough, St. Nivel's sister.

"Poor fellow!" she remarked sympathetically. "What have they been doing to you?"

I could hardly believe my eyes, and passed my hand wearily across my forehead.

St. Nivel turned to the keeper.

"Give me the brandy flask," he said.

The man produced it, and my cousin poured some out in the little silver cup attached to it.

"It's a lucky thing for you, Bill," he observed, while I greedily drank the brandy down, "that I thought of bringing this flask with me this morning. Ethel was against it; she's a total abstainer."

"Except when alcohol is needed medicinally," she interposed in an explanatory tone, "then it is another matter."

I now took a good look at her; she was wearing a short, tweed, tailor-made shooting costume, and carried in her hand a light sixteen bore shot gun.

"You look just about done," continued her brother. "Whatever has happened to you?"

"You would look bad," I answered, "if you had had nothing to eat since lunch yesterday."

St. Nivel was a soldier and man of action.

"Botley," he said to the keeper, "the sand-wiches."

"Now," said the guardsman invitingly, when I had ravenously disposed of my second sandwich, "tell us something about it."

I had just opened my lips to speak, when there came a great cry from the roof of the tower above, and a black body shot past the little window near which I was sitting.

We all ran to the window but could see nothing.

Then St. Nivel made a suggestion.

"Let us mount up to the roof," he said, "and see what is to be seen. You, Botley, had better go down to the foot of the tower."

The keeper touched his forelock and com-menced his descent of the spiral staircase. Mean-while, Lady Ethel, her brother and I mounted up to the top.

We passed the room in which I had been im-prisoned, and went up a very much narrower flight of steps to the roof, coming out at a little door which was standing open. The roof was flat and covered with lead.

"Take care how you tread," cried St. Nivel. "I expect it is all pretty rotten. In fact, Ethel, I think you had better go inside."

Ethel, however, was not of that way of thinking; she was a thorough sportswoman and wanted to see all the fun.

"All right, Jack," she rejoined cheerily. "You go on, I'll look after myself without troubling you."

It was very evident at the first glance that there had been an accident, a piece of the low stone wall which surrounded the roof was gone. It looked as if it had recently tumbled over. St. Nivel was evidently right when he said the place was rotten. Rotten it certainly was.

Stepping very gingerly we all approached the embattled wall, and, selecting the firmest part, looked over, one at a time. I had the second peep and was just in time to see two men, one limping very much – this I am sure was Saumarez – disappear into a neighbouring wood. A countrified-looking boy was running up from the opposite direction.

At the foot of the tower, however, was another matter; huddled up in a heap was the body of a man, with a coil of rope and some shattered masonry lying all around it.

By the body stood Botley, the game-keeper, scratching his head.

It was now very evident what had occurred.

The three miscreants who had tried to torture me had endeavoured to escape by letting themselves down by a rope from the top of the tower. Two had succeeded and one had been killed. The reason of this was obvious, the rope had been fixed round one of the battlements and it had not been sufficiently strong to maintain the weight of the three men. The two lowest had probably got off with a shaking, the man who had got on the rope last had lost his life. All this was perfectly evident.

"Who is it?" shouted Lord St. Nivel to the keeper below.

"Doan't know, me lord," came back the answer, "he's a stranger to me."

The keeper had now been joined by the countrified boy, and the two turned the body over on to its face. I could see that it was the fairer of the two men who had acted under Saumarez' orders.

"I think we had better go down," suggested my cousin, the Guardsman; "we may be of some service there."

On the way down the winding staircase, a thought struck me.

"What has become of that body," I asked, "that was found on Lansdown yesterday morning?"

"What body?" replied my two cousins together.

"The body of an old lady."

"We have heard nothing of it," replied St. Nivel, "and we ought to have done so. But you have not told us what happened to *you*."

Going down the old stone staircase, I gave them a brief account of my arrest in London and journey down there, with my imprisonment during the night in the tower.

"Well," remarked St. Nivel, while his sister

murmured a few words of sympathy, "I haven't quite got the hang of the thing yet, but you must tell us more at lunch."

We found that the man lying at the foot of the tower was certainly dead; his neck was broken.

We could therefore do nothing hut leave the gamekeeper in charge of the body while we despatched the boy to warn the police and fetch a doctor.

With a shilling in his pocket to get his dinner, the young yokel set off on his journey, and we strolled away.

"I don't think we'll shoot any more this morning, Jack," Ethel said, "this affair has made me feel a bit shaky."

"Then you had better come up to the house with us, Bill," said her brother, slapping me on the back, "and have some lunch. Then you can tell us all your adventures."

I readily agreed, and we had walked some little distance when I heard footsteps running behind us; we stopped and turned. It was the country boy we had sent to the police.

"I forgot to show you this yere sir," he said, opening his hand, in which he held something carefully clasped.

"What is it?" I asked as he addressed me.

"It's this yere *heye*, sir," he answered. "It don't belong to the dead 'un; he's got two."

I glanced into his open palm and beheld two halves of a brown artificial eye, made of glass, and much shot with imitation blood!

* * * * *

"No," observed my friend, Inspector Bull, "there's been no body found on Lansdown, and I should have heard of it if there had been without a doubt."

The inspector finished a liberal tumbler of Lord St. Nivel's Scotch whisky and soda, and set the tumbler carefully down on the table as if it were a piece of very rare china.

My cousin, who was standing on the hearthrug, laughed heartily.

"That was only another piece of the rogue's plot," he said. "They must have had a clever head to direct them."

"Yes," I put in, "a clever head with only one eye in it, if I'm not much mistaken."

The inspector gave me a doubtful look; then his eye reverted to the whisky decanter upon which it had been fondly fixed. St. Nivel observed it and pushed the whisky towards him.

"Thank you, my lord," said the police officer, helping himself with a look of intense satisfaction; he did not often get such whisky. "It's a curious thing, however, that this man with one eye should ha' been doing all these pranks right under my nose as it were, and I never even heard of him before."

Being aware of his methods, I was not at all surprised.

Even now, knowing that I was respectably connected, he even suspected me, and regarded me as an impostor with rich relatives.

This story of the finding of the body on Lansdown only confirmed his views of my powers of invention.

"As a matter of fact," observed Lord St. Nivel, "I am only a stranger in these parts, having borrowed a friend's house for a week's shooting; but no doubt you can tell me what this tower is, where my cousin was kept a prisoner, and which my sister and I came across by the merest chance."

"Cruft's Folly," replied the beaming inspector, with his whisky glass in his hand. "Cruft's Folly has stood where it does nearly a hundred years. It was built by some gentleman, I believe, a long while ago, to improve the landscape, just like Sham Castle over yonder."

"But does nobody live in it?"

"No, I've always understood it was quite empty and nearly a ruin."

"Then I have little doubt," said my cousin with a chuckle, "that your friends, Bill, simply appropriated it for their own uses."

"I suppose you'll have the place thoroughly searched, Mr. Bull, won't you?" I asked. "There may be something hidden there which will give you a clue to my assailants."

"You may rely upon that, Mr. Anstruther," replied the inspector, rising and slapping his chest, "but we shall have to communicate with the owner first."

Thus through the red-tapism of the law the chance was lost. Had the old tower of Cruft's Folly been searched at that moment the remainder of this history most certainly would never have been written.

Chapter VIII. Sandringham

When I got back to the comfort of the Magni-fique, though my "cure" was but half completed, yet I determined to bring my visit to Bath to a close; it had been too exciting. I would come back and finish the course of water drinking and baths some other time.

At any rate the little twinge of rheumatism in my shoulder which had brought me there was all gone. I think possibly the shocks of electricity com-bined with my agitation of mind had cured it.

St. Nivel and Lady Ethel, being tired of the "rough" shooting for the time being, and perhaps having a sneaking liking for their cousin, decided to come in to Bath and take up their quarters with me at the big hotel in the town. However, at the end of three days, being thoroughly rested, and nothing whatever having been heard of Saumarez, I decided, finally, on account of the sensation I was creating in the hotel, which was becoming an annoyance, to accept St. Nivel's invitation to put in a fortnight's shooting with him at his place in Norfolk. I had the very pleasantest recollections of it, though I had not been there for two shooting seasons.

"If you behave yourself and are very good," ex-plained Ethel, "perhaps we may take you to one of the big shoots at Sandringham. Jack is going to one, and they are always glad to have an extra gun if he happens to be such a good shot as you are."

I bowed my acknowledgments to my pretty cousin with much mock humility, but in my heart I felt very proud of the prospective honour. I had never yet occupied one of those much-coveted places in a royal shooting party. Besides, I knew that the Sandringham preserves were simply *chock-full* of pheasants and were, in fact, simply a sportsman's elysium.

"You'll be able to put in five days' shooting a week with us, Bill, if you like," St. Nivel said, "before we go over to Sandringham. My invitation is for next Thursday week, so you'll be able to get your hand in."

This gave a much-needed change to my ideas, but before I packed up to leave Bath I went down and had another look at 190 Monmouth Street.

I rang the bell and a woman opened the door with a baby in her arms.

"I'm the sergeant's wife, please sir," she said in reply to my inquiry. "We was put in here by Inspector Bull."

"Then nothing has been heard of the old lady?" I asked.

"No, sir," she replied, "nothing. The neighbours hardly knew she was here, she showed herself so seldom; but the woman that used to come in and do odd jobs for her says she's been living here ten year."

"Ten years!" I repeated in astonishment. "How on earth did she pass her time?"

"The woman says, sir, she was always writing, writing all day."

"How was she fed?" I asked anxiously. "I suppose no tradesmen called?"

"No, sir," the sergeant's wife replied, "the woman I am speaking of, who lives in the country, used to come three times a week and clean up for her, and each time she would bring her a supply of simple food, eggs and milk and such-like, to last her till she came again."

I put my hand in my pocket and gave her half a crown.

"I suppose you don't mind my looking round the house," I suggested. "I should like to see it once more before I leave Bath."

"Well," she said hesitatingly, "I'm afraid it's against orders, but – – "

The woman who hesitates is lost; she let me in.

I went with her straight down to the sitting-room. It was locked, but she had the key for cleaning purposes, and let me in.

"It looks very dreary now, don't it, sir," she queried, "in spite of all the china and finery and that?"

Yes, she was right, the room by daylight looked very dismal; the broken looking-glass over the mantelpiece did not improve its appearance.

I would have given a good deal to have been able to open the safe again if I had had the key with me and to see if it contained any further secrets, but this, for the present, was out of the question.

I had, however, the satisfaction of knowing that

the place was well guarded, and was not likely to be interfered with perhaps for years. I went into the other rooms – the sergeant and his wife were occupying the kitchens – and found nothing there but dust. One or two were locked up, but it was perfectly impossible to see what was in them. An inspection of the keyholes revealed only darkness. I came down from the top storey with a sigh at its desolation.

I left the old place and walked rather sadly down the long street back to my hotel.

I wondered as I went what had become of the poor wounded old lady; whether she had died and her body was thrust away somewhere in hiding without Christian burial, or did she by some miracle still live? But this latter suggestion seemed an utter impossibility from the state in which I had left her. So I packed up, and on the next morning, with my two cousins, left the tower of Bath Abbey behind and started *en route* for Bannington Hall, the Mid Norfolk mansion of Lord St. Nivel.

The Vanboroughs were relatives of my mother's; she was one of that noble family, and the present peer's aunt. Dear soul, she had long since gone to her rest, following my father, the Chancery Judge, in about a year after his own demise.

The Vanboroughs were celebrated for their beauty, and my mother had been no exception to the rule. My rather stern, sad features had, I suppose, come from my father, but still I think I had my mother's eyes, and a look of her about the mouth when I smiled.

At least my cousin, Ethel Vanborough, said I had.

There was always something like home about dear old Bannington to me, with a sniff of the sea when you first stepped out of the carriage at the door.

The big comfortable old landau with its pair of strong horses had now, however, given place to a smart motor car, upholstered like a little drawing-room.

My cousin, Lord St. Nivel, was certainly fully up to date, and his sister, Lady Ethel, was, if possible, a little more so. They were twins. Left orphans as children, the two had grown up greatly attached to one another naturally, and being the sole survivors of a very rich family and inheriting all its savings and residues, they had an extremely good time of it together without any great desire to exchange their happy brother and sisterhood for the bonds of matrimony. Still they were very young, being only four-and-twenty.

I spent a very happy ten days with them in the glorious old mansion full of recollections and relics of bygone ages. Its very red brick peacefulness had a soothing effect upon me, and I will defy any one to experience greater comfort than we did coming in tired out after a day's tramp after the partridges – for St. Nivel was an advocate of "rough" shooting – and sitting round the great blazing fire of logs in the hall while Ethel poured out our tea.

I will admit that Ethel and I indulged in a mild

flirtation; we always did when we met, especially when we had not seen one another for some time, which was the case in the present instance.

Still it was only a *cousinly* flirtation and never went beyond a pressure of the hand, or on very rare occasions a kiss, when we met by chance perhaps, in the gloaming of the evening, in one of the long, old world corridors, when no one was about.

Shooting almost every day, I soon got back into my old form again.

"Yes, you'll do," remarked my cousin, when I brought down my seventh "rocketter," in succession the day before the royal shoot. "If you shoot like that to-morrow, Bill, you'll be asked to Sandringham again!"

A few words from my cousin to the courteous old secretary had gained me the invitation I so desired; I was determined to do my very best to keep up my reputation as a good sporting shot. We motored over the next morning; Ethel with us. It was always understood that St. Nivel's invitations included her, in fact, she was a decided favourite in the royal circle, and being an expert photographer, handy with her snapshotter, always had something interesting to talk about when she came across the Greatest Lady.

We found the members of the shooting party lounging about the terrace, for the most part smoking and waiting for their host. Several motor cars were in readiness to carry them off to the various plantations.

Presently our host arrived, and we were complete; I heard him remark to one of the guests as he got into his car –

"There are three more of those lazy fellows to arrive," he said, laughing, "but they must come on by themselves in another car."

Our first shot was on the Wolverton Road about half-way down towards the station, and here the birds were as plentiful as blackberries. I never before had seen such a head of game. The beaters entered the plantations in a row, standing close together, and moved *one step* at a time, each step sending out perhaps a dozen pheasants, who were, as a rule, quickly disposed of by the guns around.

Of course there were exceptions: there were those who missed their birds both barrels time after time, or still worse sent them away sorely wounded with their poor shattered legs hanging helplessly down.

These were the sort of shots who were not required at Sandringham, and, as a rule, were not asked again. I, however, was fortunate; being in good practice and cool, I brought down my birds one after the other, as St. Nivel remarked afterwards, "like a bit of clockwork," and I had the satisfaction of hearing our host inquire who I was. We had finished one plantation very satisfactorily, as the heaps of dead pheasants testified, and were moving off to the next when I got a shock.

A motor car came rushing on to the road, and stopped quite near to where I was strolling along in conversation with one of the equerries.

"Ah! you lazy fellows!" exclaimed our host, "you are losing all the best of the sport."

A well-known foreign nobleman, a tall, dark, handsome fellow, got out first and advanced full of apologies, hat in hand.

My glance was fixed upon his very prepossessing face and I did not at the moment notice the gentleman who followed him. When I did I started violently and the equerry walking with me asked what was the matter.

"Nothing is the matter particularly," I answered, passing my hand before my eyes, "but can you tell me the name of that gentleman who has just got out of the car?"

"You mean the red-faced man with the black imperial?" he suggested.

"Yes," I answered.

"Oh! That is some Bavarian duke," he answered, "not royal, but a Serene Somebody. I forget his name myself, but I will ask some one, and tell you."

A friend in the Household was passing at the time and he caught his arm and whispered him a question.

"Yes, of course," he said, turning again to me; "he is the Duke Rittersheim, one of those small German principalities swept away long ago, and of which only the title and the family estates remain."

I turned and took another look at His Serene

Highness. Yes, Duke of Rittersheim or not, the red-faced, dark-haired foreigner, who was advancing half cringingly, hat in hand and full of apologies, was none other than Saumarez, the man who had tried to torture me in the tower of Cruft's Folly!

Chapter IX. The Duke of Rittersheim

That little *rencontre* took my nerve away, and I shot very badly at the next plantation, so badly – I missed two birds – that I was almost inclined to give up and go home; but then lunch came – in a marquee – and its luxury and the delightful wine restored me. I shot well again all the afternoon.

Yes, it was a glorious day, and I enjoyed it immensely when I got Saumarez – or His Serene Highness – out of my mind. He was a superb shot, I will say that of him; he fired from the left shoulder as many men do, but in his case I knew it was on account of his glass eye.

Walking to the last plantation with one of the Household and casually discussing all manner of ordinary subjects, I ventured a chance remark concerning the Duke of Rittersheim.

"His Serene Highness is a fine shot," I said, "an old sportsman, it is easy to see."

"Yes," answered my companion, "he is supposed to be one of the finest shots in Germany."

"And yet he has a glass eye?" I ventured.

The man I was walking with turned round and stared at me.

"Now, how in the name of goodness did you know that?" he inquired. "It is supposed to be a secret, and the artificial eye looks so natural under his pince-nez that very few know of its existence."

"But you are quite right," he continued; "he lost

it in a shooting accident when he was a boy."

This made the matter quite certain in my mind, and I determined to confront His Serene Highness at the first opportunity and see what effect it would have upon him; but I might have saved myself the trouble of this resolution; subsequent event proved pretty conclusively that he had recognised me from the first.

We were all arranged for the final shoot of the day, when to my astonishment I found myself next to the Duke of Rittersheim. He was on my right hand, and therefore had me well under his sound left eye.

I must admit that I felt uneasy when I saw him there; nevertheless, I went on shooting coolly and had the pleasure once or twice of "wiping his eye." I even heard a distinct "Bravo" come from him at one of my shots.

I was, however, far from comfortable in having him for such a close neighbour under the circumstances, and wished him a hundred miles away. We shot on until the light got very bad, but there were only a few more yards to be driven, so we went on. We had nearly finished when I noticed the Duke of Rittersheim send his loader away to pick up something he had dropped.

I noted the man run off to fulfil the request, and at the same moment my eyes were attracted by the last rays of the red sun, already set, reddening far away the waters of Lynn Deeps.

It was a lovely sight, and my gaze rested on it

some moments; then I suddenly realised that I was practically alone with the Bavarian Duke, as my loader had walked on a few yards with his back to me.

The Duke was standing quite alone, and in that moment I saw his gun go up to his shoulder at a bird, then in a flash it turned towards me!

I realised my danger in a moment and threw myself flat on my face. As I lay there I heard the report of his gun, the swish of the charge, and a cry from my loader. He had shot him!

I sprang to my feet, and ran to the man, who was standing holding his arm; but quick as I was the Duke was there before me.

"Are you hurt, my man?" he asked in his sharp tone which I knew so well. "Where are you hit?"

"It's in the arm, sir," the Norfolk man answered; "it be set fast."

"Look here," said the Duke, quickly taking out a note case. "I can see you are not badly hurt. Take these bank-notes; here are twenty pounds. Go quietly away and say nothing about it and I'll give you another twenty. Do you understand?"

"Yes, me lord," answered the man, who probably had never had so much money before in his life. "I'll keep mum."

"Can you walk all right?" asked the Duke.

"Yes, Your Royal Highness," answered the poor fellow, who was getting mixed, feeling, no doubt, very faint.

"Then off with you at once," cried the Duke, "and send some one up in the morning to the Duke of Rittersheim for the other twenty pounds. Tell the people," he added, as the man went slowly off, "that you have had a bad fall."

"Yes, Your Majesty," answered the bewildered, wounded man as he disappeared in the dusk.

I stood watching the Duke as he went coolly back without a word to me to his place; this, then, was the cool, resourceful scoundrel I had to deal with!

* * * * *

Sitting by the big fire in the smoking-room at Bannington Hall that night after dinner, I told St. Nivel the whole of the incident of the shooting of the beater by the Duke of Rittersheim.

"Well, that's the limit," commented Jack, taking the cigar out of his mouth; "he *must* be a cool-headed scoundrel. I never heard of such nerve!"

"It's a nice thing to have a brute like that on one's track, isn't it?" I remarked dejectedly; "it makes life hardly worth living."

Jack sat and smoked placidly for some moments looking into the fire. He was thinking.

Presently he turned to me.

"Look here, Bill," he remarked, "Ethel and I had a talk this evening before dinner about matters generally and she has started what I call a very good idea."

"What's that?" I asked.

"Of course, she knows all about your promise to the old lady; you told her, you know."

"Certainly," I answered, "I told you both. I know you never keep secrets from one another."

"Well, she knows," he proceeded, "therefore, that you have made up your mind to go to Valoro with that packet the old lady gave you."

"Well?"

Jack brought his hand down with a smack on my knee.

"Let us come too, old chap," he cried – "both of us – Ethel and I."

The idea to me was both pleasant and astonishing. I had never thought of it.

"But won't Ethel find it rather a fatiguing journey?" I suggested.

He was quite amused at the idea.

"I can assure you," he said, "that she can stand pretty nearly as much as I can. She's a regular little amazon. That's what Ethel is."

"Very well, then," I replied, "nothing will suit me better than to have yours and Ethel's charming society. As a matter of fact I am beginning to look forward to the expedition keenly."

The next few days were given up to wild speculations on our coming journey and its results.

"I hear the country is lovely," exclaimed Ethel, poring over a map; "at any rate the voyage will be splendid!"

It was settled that we should start from Liverpool to Monte Video, thence make our way by rail across country to our destination, Valoro, a beautiful city in the mountains of Aquazilia, in the neighbourhood of which we were told we should get splendid sport.

Therefore we made a flying trip to town, especially to visit Purdey's and supply ourselves with the very latest things in sporting guns and rifles.

Out of the very liberal provision the old lady had made for my expenses, I felt justified in being extravagant, and provided myself with a beautiful gun – the right barrel having a shallow rifling for a bullet should we meet with very big game – and a perfect gem of an express rifle; these two were the latest models in sporting firearms.

Ethel and St. Nivel, having an unlimited command of money, ordered pretty nearly everything they were advised to take, with the result that we required a small pantechnicon van to take our combined luggage.

There was, however, one thing I was very particular about, and upon which I took the advice of an old friend who had travelled much.

I bought a first-rate *Target* revolver – a Colt –

with which I knew I could make *accurate* shooting. I would not trust my life to one of those unscientific productions which are just as likely to shoot a friend as an enemy, and are more in the nature of pop-guns than defensive weapons. I had reason to congratulate myself later on that I had taken such a precaution.

"There's one thing you really must see to at once, Bill," exclaimed St. Nivel, one day when we were all busy making out lists of our requirements in the great library and posting them off to the stores. "You *must* get a servant."

Now I had been, for the last three months, doing for myself; my old servant had left me some months before and I had not filled his place with another. Times, too, had not been very prosperous with me and I seriously thought of curtailing that luxury and brushing my own clothes.

The liberal allowance for my travelling expenses, however, plus the thousand pound note, put quite a different complexion on matters. I felt now thoroughly justified in providing myself with a first-rate man, and for that purpose I took my cousin's advice and put an advertisement in the *Morning Post.*

"A gentleman requires a good valet, used to travelling. Excellent reference required." I gave my name and St. Nivel's address to ensure getting a good one.

That was the wording of it, and I arranged to run up to town for a day to make my selection from them. From the numerous applicants I selected six, and told them to meet me at Long's Hotel.

St. Nivel accompanied me to give me the benefit of his advice, which was perhaps not likely to be of much service to me. He employed a refined person himself who asked and got £150 a year.

The man who took my fancy was an old cavalry soldier named Brooks who had been out of work for a time, but who yet bore the stamp of a man who knew his work and would do it. I closed with him for a modest £70 a year, and he was glad to get it.

"When will you be ready to come, Brooks?" I asked when we had settled preliminaries. "We shall be off by the next boat to La Plata, and I shall want you to get on with the packing as soon as you can."

"For the matter of that, sir," he answered, "I could come now. I've no chick nor child to hold me. I'm a widower without encumbrances."

I told the "widower without encumbrances" to come the next day, and St. Nivel and I jumped into a hansom to catch the five o'clock express, glad to get out of the thick atmosphere of London into the bright crisp air of Norfolk.

"I think you've done right," remarked St. Nivel in the train, "in getting an old cavalry man. He'll understand hunting things."

As I could not afford to hunt I missed the point of the signification.

Ah, those were happy days, those last few before we started!

All our serious preparations were finished and we had only to give a little general supervision to the packing of our respective servants. Ethel's experienced maid was going with her, of course.

This done, we used to stroll about together – the three of us – and enjoy the last few hours of the dear old place as much as we could in the beautiful bright weather.

I think Ethel and I even used to get a little bit romantic in the lovely moonlight nights, when the old oak-panelled corridors and staircases were bathed in the soft light. But we were very far from being in love with one another all the same.

I shall never forget that time of peace, which came in a period of storm and trial; the old red mansion with the river running not a hundred yards from it, and the graceful swans sailing to and fro, the glorious old trees of the avenue, the fine broad terrace with its splendid views over the low, undulating country, with a glimpse of Lynn Deeps on one hand and the white towers of St. Margaret's, the great church in the ancient town, on the other.

The dreamy, old-world air of the place, the smell even of the fresh-turned earth in the great gardens, the cawing of the circling rooks – it all comes back to me as if I had but walked out of it all an hour ago.

However, the morning soon came when we were to bid adieu to it all, and in the hurry and scurry of it and the race down to the station in the motor – for we were late, Ethel's maid having forgotten an important hat – perhaps we forgot all our peaceful happiness in our feverish speculations on our voyage across the Atlantic to that distant South American Republic, Aquazilia, and its mountain capital, Valoro.

Chapter X. The Plot that Failed

Settling on the Hotel Victoria as our headquarters, we prepared to make the two days before our sailing as amusing as possible, but I always had before me the nightmare of the little carved casket which I was to carry with me.

I decided I would take no risks with it. I would go and fetch it from my solicitors on the afternoon of our departure, on the way to the station. It was very evident to me that this casket contained something of the greatest possible interest to several people, including in particular His Serene Highness, the Duke of Rittersheim.

When, then, Ethel, St. Nivel and I had crowded all the visits to theatres and matinees we could into the intervening two days, we sat taking our last luncheon in England, probably, for some time to come.

"I am so glad we are going by this boat instead of the next," remarked St. Nivel, taking a glass of Chartreuse from the attentive waiter who was on the look out for a parting tip; "a fortnight makes all the difference in that part of the world; we shall just get there for the tail end of the summer, which they say is glorious. A bit of a change, I am thinking," he added, with a glance out of the window, "to this kind of diluted pea-soup weather we get here in November."

"Let us see," said Ethel, with a calculating air, "this is the last week in November. We arrive there the second week in December, and the rainy season does not begin until the middle of January. We shall have a clear month to enjoy ourselves in!"

"Very delightful," I replied; "a delightful voyage under delightful circumstances."

I bowed to my cousin Ethel as I raised my liqueur glass to my lips.

She blew away the smoke of the cigarette she took from hers – we were in a private room – and smiled at me.

"You flattering old courtier!" she answered; "you get those airs through writing romances. What is more to the purpose, have you secured those three state cabins on the C deck of the *Oceana*?"

"Well," I answered laconically, "I've paid the money for them at any rate. Sixty-six pounds the three, over and above first-class fare!"

"And very cheap, too," replied Ethel; "the comfort of sleeping in a real brass bedstead instead of those intolerable bunks is worth three times as much!"

I looked at my cigar and said nothing; but for the generosity of the old lady of Monmouth Street, Bath, a bunk would have been my lot, without doubt, in the ordinary way. Though she had laid a heavy burden upon me, she certainly had a kind consideration for my comfort.

Further conversation was put an end to by the entry of my new man, Brooks, with my travelling coat.

"The motor's at the door, sir," he announced.

I had engaged a special motor-brougham to take me from the hotel to my lawyers in Lincoln's Inn, and from there to the station with the precious casket in my possession; I had already banked the notes. I wished to make the journey as rapidly as possible, and Brooks was to accompany me, my luggage going on under the care of St. Nivel's man.

"Then *au revoir* until we meet at Euston," I said to my cousins; "mind you are in good time for the train."

"We shall be all right," answered Ethel. "I wish we were coming with you. I feel rather anxious about you."

"Don't you worry, Ethel," St. Nivel replied, "he'll be all right. He's not a child."

I went off and got into the motor, Brooks taking his seat on the box.

We rattled away through the crowded streets in the dim half-fog that was enveloping the town, and duly arrived at the dreary-looking offices of the lawyers.

There I did not lose a minute; they had been duly apprised of my coming and I found Watson the managing clerk already waiting for me.

"Here are the two packets, Mr. Anstruther," he said, handing them to me; "they are just as you left them, you see, and the seals are intact."

I examined them and found them quite correct.

"What a fortunate thing," added Watson, as I buttoned my overcoat over the pocket in which I had stowed the little parcels, "that I saw you push those two packets into the pigeon-holes, and stopped that scoundrel from laying his hands on them!"

"Yes, it was a very lucky thing," I replied, "and I am very much obliged to you for your promptness in gathering my meaning."

"Yes, it was a fortunate escape for you, sir," he added; "when I saw you go away with those two men, I never felt more miserable in my life. But, of course, we read all about the truth of it next afternoon in the evening paper. One can hardly believe such things possible in these times with our efficient police."

"Ye-es," – I hesitated, with my mind on the thick necks and whisky-drinking proclivities of some of the "'tecs" I had known, – "I suppose we can never rely upon *absolute* safety in this world."

Then as I spoke a thought struck me; I noticed that the packets were rather bulging out in the pocket in which I had placed them. I had an idea I would change their position. I quickly took them out and placed one in each of my trousers pockets; there was then nothing in my appearance to denote where they were. In the result, it was a very lucky thing I had taken this precaution.

To preserve the secret of their whereabouts, I kept my hand in the breast of my travelling coat as if I were guarding the precious parcels there, and in this way I left the lawyers' office and made for the motor-brougham, the door of which was being held open by my man Brooks.

Just as I was half-way across the pavement, a man selling evening papers came rushing by and shouting –

"'Orrible murder! Suicide of the assassin! 'Orrible murder!"

He was running very fast and apparently not looking where he was going, for he knocked roughly against me as he passed, dislodging my hand from my breast; but Brooks he ran right into, full tilt, with the result that my man lost his balance and sprawled on the pavement.

It was then that a very fussy little over-dressed man came bustling up out of the fog, accompanied by a very attractive lady.

"A more disgraceful thing, sir," he said, addressing me, "I have never seen before. I trust you are not hurt, sir?"

"No, thank you, I'm all right," I answered, half inclined to laugh at Brooks scrambling up from the pavement and brushing himself, for it was a wet, slimy day and the pavements muddy. The newspaper man had disappeared.

"Why, I declare," exclaimed the little man, "the scamp has covered you with mud!"

I looked down; there certainly was a splash of mud on the front of my coat. I wondered how it had got there. Despite my assertions, the two – both the lady and the gentleman – insisted on brushing me, until in very desperation I had to get into the brougham out of their way. Then they suddenly made me very polite bows and disappeared.

Brooks mounted the box, and we rattled away to Euston. There was one thing which attracted my attention, however, on that short journey. Brooks' ungloved hand was hanging down as he sat on the box, and I noticed that he kept snapping his fingers as he sat.

"That's a very highly nervous man," I said to myself, "and even that little incident has upset him."

Brooks' nervousness passed out of my mind altogether when we reached Euston, and I sought in the bustle for my two cousins. I found them at last standing in front of the reserved coupé which I had taken care to have secured for us by my man.

When they saw me, a look of surprise and amusement came over their faces, and they both laughed heartily.

"What on earth have you been doing, Will?" Ethel cried. "Have you been to a suffragists' meeting on the way?"

Ethel affected to laugh at the suffragists, but in her heart I believe she would have liked to join them, and perhaps would have done so but for her brother.

"No," I answered; "what's the matter with me?"

"Look at your coat," replied St. Nivel, pointing to the breast of that garment.

I did look, and found that both my travelling

coat and the coat underneath it had been cut completely through the left breast, where my pocket was, with a knife whose edge must have been as keen as that of a razor.

At the first shock I cried, half aloud –

"Good God! The packets have been stolen."

Then I recollected my forethought in placing them in my trousers pockets, and I dived my hands into them instinctively. Yes, thank God, they were all right; my two hands closed on their crisp sealed surfaces.

But how had it occurred?

I thought of the man tearing along with the evening papers, the upsetting of Brooks, and the fussy lady and gentleman who had insisted on brushing me down. I saw it all now – a carefully prepared plan!

Then I roared with laughter, much to the astonishment of Ethel and St. Nivel.

"They've had all their trouble for nothing," I gasped, simply stamping with delight; "the silly fools have got nothing!" But I was wrong; they had got my brand new cigar case given me by Ethel with my initials on it and full of St. Nivel's best Havannahs, placed there by her own fair hands for the railway journey.

Chapter XI. The Oceana

Very thankful were my two cousins and I when we got clear of the fogs of the Mersey and were fairly out at sea. Not that we were bad sailors. We did not proclaim that we were, at any rate, though I will admit that for the first two days I found my comfortable brass bedstead a resting-place much more to my liking than a seat at the dinner-table, although I duly turned up there for the sake of appearances. During this period of seclusion I thought deeply of the latest attempt of my enemies to secure the casket, and it caused me great uneasiness. I could not imagine how they knew that I should go to my lawyers for it.

Ethel made a brave show, but it was quite the third day out from Liverpool before I saw her smile as I wished to see her smile – without a mental reservation, in fact.

St. Nivel was really the only perfectly unconcerned member of our party, and it was through his persevering attendances on the promenade deck, that I became acquainted with a young lady who will figure largely in these pages, although she in reality was by no means of commanding stature, but one of those charming petite persons whose mission in life appears to be to exemplify what extraordinarily choice pieces of human goods can be made up in small parcels.

It was on the fourth day out that I became acquainted with Dolores d'Alta. While I had been lying disconsolately on my cot, St. Nivel had been improving the shining hour by looking after Miss Dolores, who had taken up her position, during the first few days of her trial, in a sheltered position on the promenade deck, in preference to her "stuffy cabin," as she called her state room.

It had been the pleasure, and had become the duty – a self-imposed one – of St. Nivel to see that she was properly wrapped up.

She did not object to smoke either, having, as she stated, been brought up in an atmosphere of smoke at home. Therefore Jack smoked his cigar.

Had I not known that St. Nivel's inclinations were apparently fixed in the direction of bachelor-hood, I should have thought he had fallen in love; but I discovered later that he had, to use an expression of his own, "simply taken on another pal." He found her a congenial person in whose society to smoke cigars. But if he had fallen in love, certainly he would have had a most excellent excuse for doing so.

A daintier little specimen of Southern beauty it would have been difficult to imagine than this little Aquazilian aristocrat. To describe her in a few words, she was a beautiful woman in miniature; she was the most perfectly symmetrical little piece of womanhood that I had ever set eyes upon.

A perfectly clear, creamy complexion, yet not without colour of a rose tint; dimples in the cheeks, which were ravishing when she smiled, – and she was very fond of smiling, ay, and laughing too, and showing the most perfect set of white teeth, – black hair, and very dark blue eyes; and there you have her. United to this beauty of person was a most fascinating natural manner; not the manner of a flirt, but that of a light-hearted, pure-minded girl, as gay as a lark released from captivity, and not unlike it in its new freedom, for she had not escaped from a first-rate finishing school in Paris more than six months.

She had spent the intervening period under the care of a sister of her father who had married an Englishman and who lived in good society.

She had had a season in London and had spent the autumn in a round of country visits which accounted for her wonderful *savoir faire*; she was only eighteen. Now she was going home to her dear father, a widower, under the care of her aunt. Hearing her always referred to in conversation as "Dolores," her surname was a revelation when I heard it properly pronounced. St. Nivel's idea of foreign names was exceedingly hazy and misleading. As soon as she told me she was going home to Aquazilia, I became very alert and began to ask her questions.

"Yes," she replied to my query concerning her parent's name, "my father is the Senor Don Juan d'Alta; in the old time of our monarchy he was for many years the Prime Minister. He is a very old man is my father," she further explained; "he is nearly seventy!"

Looking at her I could understand the old man simply making an idol of this his only child. It appeared to me very marvellous that I should have met her.

Some of the other passengers told me that he was a member of one of the oldest and most aristocratic families in the country.

It was very lovely as we steamed farther and farther away from our own cold fogs and got into the warmth of the south; very fascinating to walk on deck with Dolores and talk, under the brilliant stars, of Aquazilia and the extraordinary chance which had made us meet on board both with the same destination in view – the house of her father.

"I don't think, though, it is so strange," she confided to me one lovely moonlight night when we were walking the promenade deck side by side; "it is not an unreasonable thing that we should have taken the same boat, considering that they only run once a fortnight."

"It is certainly not unreasonable," I answered, with a look into her eyes. "It is the most reasonable chance that I have ever come across in the whole of my life!"

"Why?" she answered, with a look of mischief in her dark blue eyes.

"Because," I answered fervently, with a little tremor in my voice, "it has given me the chance of spending three weeks near you!

"Let us go and look at the flying fish," she answered hastily, to change the conversation. "I do so love to see them."

Yes, I was daily becoming more and more attached to her; for the first time in my long career of flirtation I was beginning to find out what love *really* meant.

I was falling in love with a little divinity twelve years my junior, and from the depths of my knowledge I expected she would very justly make a fool of me – not intentionally, perhaps, but in effect the same – and laugh at me for my pains.

It seemed very bitter to think of as I saw her walking – and laughing and talking too – with St. Nivel who was six years my junior. It seemed to me, in my growing jealousy, an ideal match for her.

I forgot that young ladies never fall in love with the persons they are expected to, but invariably go off on an unknown tangent of their own, in obedience to the same law of Nature, perhaps, which causes an unusually tall girl to lose her heart to a very diminutive – though generally very consequential – little man.

In the contemplation of the varied charms of Dolores d'Alta, I almost forgot my precious casket, confided in fear and trembling to the care of the captain, and locked up by him in the ship's strong room in my presence and in the presence of St. Nivel.

In due course we came to Coruña, or Corunna as we more commonly call it, and there I had the delight of strolling about the old fortifications all alone with Dolores and showing her the tomb of Sir John Moore, while St. Nivel obligingly took charge of her aunt, and solicitously kept her out of earshot. The old lady had lived long enough in England to appreciate the attentions of a lord, and he a rich one, without designs on her niece's fortune.

Yes, that fortune was my stumbling-block; I learned of it from old Sir Rupert Frampton, our minister to Aquazilia, who was travelling back to his post on the *Oceana*.

"I really don't suppose," he said, one evening in the smoking-room, nodding his head sententiously, "that old Don Juan d'Alta knows what he is worth; neither do I suppose that he cares much, for he is a man of the simplest tastes, living on the plainest food, and having but one hobby and object, in fact, in life."

"His daughter?" I suggested at once, Dolores, of course, being the uppermost thought in my mind.

"No," replied the old gentleman crisply, with the smartness of the *diplomat*; "reptiles!"

"Reptiles!" I exclaimed in disgust; "what reptiles?"

"Principally snakes," replied the old man, shifting his cigar in his mouth; "he has a regular Zoological Gardens full of them – all kinds, from boa-constrictors to adders. He makes pets of them."

"Not about the *house*?" I suggested.

"No, not exactly," Sir Rupert replied, "unless they stray in by themselves. He's very eccentric and I don't think has been quite himself since the queen abdicated. They say he was in love with her, notwithstanding the fact that she was a confirmed old maid."

"Indeed," I replied, curious to keep the old man talking, for I was desirous of hearing as much as I possibly could about Aquazilia and its capital, Valoro, "it sounds quite romantic."

"Well, it *was* romantic in a way," he proceeded, glad to have a listener, as old men are; "there's always a certain amount of romance about the court of a reigning queen. Of course you know that the Salic law did not prevail in the kingdom of Aquazilia when it *was* a kingdom. Yes, it was a splendid court was that of Valoro when Her Majesty Inez the Second reigned over it. I just remember it thirty-five years ago when I went out to it as a young attaché on one of my first appointments and took such a fancy to the lovely country."

"Then it *is* lovely," I ventured; "the reports of it are not exaggerations?"

Old Sir Rupert replied almost with emotion –

"It is superb. It is the loveliest country in the world!"

"In those days I am speaking of," he proceeded, "Valoro was a place worth living in. In many respects it outshone some of the courts of Europe, with which, by the bye, it was in close contact. Queen Inez, as you no doubt know, was a Princess of Istria; the royal line of Aquazilia was simply a collateral branch of the great Imperial House of Dolphberg. And there were those that said that Queen Inez despite all her resistance of the many endeavours to induce her to enter the married state – and her offers had been abundant – was not only a queen and a rich one, but she was also a very beautiful woman."

"Your account of Queen Inez, Sir Rupert, is absolutely fascinating," I said. "I am almost inclined to fall in love with her. Where is she now?"

The old man paused and a sad look came over his face.

"She is dead, poor woman," he answered sadly; "they say she died of a broken heart."

"At losing the throne?" I queried.

"I don't know, I'm sure," he said slowly, throwing away the end of his cigar. "Some say she was glad to get rid of the responsibilities of it, and quite content to retire to a castle she had in Switzerland not far from the Lake of Lucerne. She was a woman of very simple tastes."

"It seems a pity she did not marry," I suggested, "as far as one can judge."

"Well, it is highly probable," he answered, "that she would not have lost her throne if she had had a husband to stand up for her. She was no match for Razzaro."

"Who was Razzaro?" I asked.

"Well, he was the sort of adventurer," the old diplomat answered, "that South America seems especially to breed. He was a man of great talents and abandoned to unscrupulousness. I believe he would have sold his own mother, if he could have got a good bid, and would have haggled with the purchaser whether the price was to include the clothes she stood in."

"A thoroughly honourable, straightforward gentleman," I suggested ironically. "I can imagine a lady such as you describe Queen Inez to have been being peculiarly unfitted to deal with such a man!"

"Yes," agreed Sir Rupert; "and her Prime Minister, or Chancellor as they called him, Don Juan d'Alta, was not much better. He had the misfortune to possess the nature of a modern Bayard, and believed in everybody, until he found out too late that he had been deceived. That is how Queen Inez lost her throne. Razzaro was slowly but surely sapping the Royal power for years, right under d'Alta's nose, and he never really found it out until the whole country burst into revolution."

"What happened then?" I asked.

"Nothing happened," replied Sir Rupert. "When the Queen discovered that the voice of the people was in favour of a Republic she simply abdicated. She would not allow a drop of blood to be shed in her behalf. An Istrian warship which had been waiting for her at the coast took her to Europe with her devoted lady-in-waiting, the Baroness d'Altenberg."

"D'Altenberg," I muttered; "where have heard that name?"

"It was a bloodless revolution."

"And Razzaro triumphed?" I added aloud.

"Yes; Razzaro triumphed," he replied; "and, as a matter of fact, thoroughly got hold of the popular favour. His son is President of the Republic at the present moment. Old Razzaro made a sort of family living of the Presidency."

"And Don Juan d'Alta retired into private life?" I ventured.

"Into private life and the society of his reptiles," added the old diplomatist, rising. "I think the latter have consoled him for many disappointments."

"Whom did he marry?" I asked.

"A very beautiful French lady," he replied, "whose husband, a French nobleman, had come to Aquazilia to try and make his fortune, and had died in the effort."

"Poor man!" I commented. "And Don Juan married his widow?"

"Exactly; and this pretty little lady, Señorita Dolores, who is returning to Valoro with us, is the result of the union. They say she is the very image of her mother, who died when she was five."

"Then the mother must have been very beautiful," was my comment.

The old minister stopped and looked at me for some moments without saying anything. Then, with a peculiar smile about the corners of his good-natured mouth, shook his head and went slowly out of the smoking-room.

Chapter XII. Held Up

Rio with its heat, its tramways, and its great sea wall; its Botanical Gardens in which once more I had the delight of losing myself with Dolores, to the evident anxiety of her aunt and duenna, Mrs. Darbyshire; it seemed so strange to find such a foreign little person with such a distinctly English name. She, however, refused to be beguiled away by St. Nivel to look at the giraffes. I think she began to smell more than a rat when we reached the monkey house, and to doubt whether his attentions to her were as disinterested as they appeared, especially when she heard that I was his cousin.

To marry his poor relation – me – to a rich heiress – her niece Dolores – no doubt struck her as an end worth taking some trouble about. Probably she would have done the same herself.

Therefore as we approached our port of debarkation, after leaving Rio, I began to find my little interviews with Dolores becoming restricted more often by the presence of her aunt. Still the recollection of our rambles at Rio, and the rides alone on the tops of the electric trams – which are quite orthodox – remained with us; and if Mrs. Darbyshire became more severe, were there not those little stolen interviews in the dark part of the promenade deck, where the electric light did not reach, worth a lifetime; and did I not day by day have that growing feeling round my heart, which thrilled me through and through and told me that my little darling was beginning to care for me?

Did she not absolutely shed tears the night we stole away from the concert and sat hand in hand under one of the boats, when I whispered just one little sentence; that I loved her? Ah me! shall I ever forget those beautiful Southern nights, with the stars shining like great diamonds above us – nights made for love?

My cousin Ethel at first did not by any means appreciate the turn my affections had recently taken; she made several pointed and rather sarcastic remarks about it, having in her mind, I presume, the recollection of our little meetings in the long corridors of dear old Bannington.

"You seem very much taken up with that Miss d'Alta," she remarked one day. "I thought you did not like foreign girls. I don't suppose she can ride or shoot a bit."

"I don't want her to, Ethel," I replied tersely; "there are no facilities for either amusement on board ship."

She smiled, then bit her lips to check it; she wanted to be dignified and couldn't. She descended to mere abuse.

"You were always a fool about girls, Bill," she continued. "Any girl could twist you round her finger. Do you remember Mary Greenway?"

Now the recollection of that young lady was peculiarly galling to me at the moment. After expressing deep love for me – I was eighteen – for nearly six months, she eloped with one of her father's grooms!

"Please don't mention that young lady," I implored; "it makes me feel ill. I believe at the present moment she teaches young ladies in her husband's riding-school."

Ethel laughed heartily.

"She might do worse," she replied. "I think she is rather a plucky girl."

"What, to run away with a groom?" I suggested.

"No," she snapped; "to work for her living."

We came to our port of debarkation, Monte Video, at last. It seemed like the end of a holiday to go ashore, and take to the dusty train, luxurious though it was, but *now* I had the precious casket in my care, and the anxiety was almost too much for me.

"Look here," said St. Nivel, when we had been in the train about an hour, "you are looking pretty sick over that precious packet, why don't you let me take care of it for you?"

I tapped nervously at the trousers pocket in which I was carrying it.

"I hardly like to let it go out of my own charge," I answered anxiously; "though I know, of course, that it would be safe with you."

We were, at the time of this conversation, running through a most beautiful valley, glorious with tropical vegetation. The train was gradually rising on an easy gradient to the higher lands, where we hoped to get fresher air, for the heat in the valley was most oppressive after three weeks passed practically in the open on the deck of the *Oceana*.

Without in any way forcing myself on Mrs. Darbyshire's society, I contrived to see a good deal of Dolores on this little railway journey, which was only to occupy a day and a half.

Once on the beautiful tableland with its gorgeous views of hill and dale, ocean and distant mountain, the train sped onwards at a rate almost alarming to us used to the slower methods of Europe.

It was well on in the evening; we had dined excellently in the well-provided restaurant car, and were lounging about in the moonlight thinking of turning in – for there were several sleeping-cars attached to the train – when the incident occurred which very nearly rendered my journey fruitless. It was just as we had entered Aquazilian territory, and passed the customs. We were, as I have said, lounging about smoking, when the train which was running through a deep cutting suddenly slowed down, and presently the breaks were put on so hard that we who were standing near were nearly thrown off our feet.

"Whatever is the matter?" cried Ethel, who was sitting in a compartment of the smoking-car with us. "I hope there is no accident."

St. Nivel, who was sitting opposite to me, suddenly leaned forward and whispered –

"If you have that packet of yours handy, give it to me. I think there will be trouble."

He had travelled in America before, and I placed a good deal of reliance on his experience.

From the front of the train there arose a great hubbub, a chorus of exclamations in Spanish.

"I thought so," remarked St. Nivel; "you'd better look sharp, Bill, if you want to make that packet safe."

As he spoke, he held out towards me an open cigar-box which he had taken out of the rack.

Then I saw what he was aiming at; he wished me for some reason to hide my packet among the cigars in the box.

I did not hesitate a moment, but put my hand in my trousers pocket, and pulling out the precious packet, placed it among the cigars.

He immediately covered it with more cigars, and then put the box back in the rack.

There was a sudden stillness in the front of the train, and I saw through the windows of the smok-ing-car quite a cloud of horsemen ride up the per-manent way and dismount; apparently the forepart of the train had been already occupied, for we heard the sound of a by no means unpleasant voice making in English the following request: –

"Hands up, gentlemen."

I was unused to this sort of thing, but St. Nivel apparently knew all about it, for he sat back in his seat with a curse between his teeth.

"What does it mean?" asked Ethel and I, almost

113

in a breath.

"It means," answered St. Nivel, "that we are going to be robbed."

"Oh, my God!" cried poor Ethel, "I hope they won't murder us!"

By the white look on St. Nivel's face, as he sat with his teeth set, I saw that there was something in his mind which he feared for his sister more than death.

I knew afterwards what some of these South American half-bred freebooters were like.

The men who had ridden up by the side of the train were a queer-looking lot.

For the most part they wore very loose garments and high-crowned hats, somewhat of the kind worn by Guy Fawkes. Slung at the saddle of each man was a coil of rope – a lasso. Nearly every one of them carried a rifle.

"I shall get my revolver," I exclaimed. "I've left it in my dressing-bag."

"Do nothing of the sort," cried St. Nivel, in alarm; "they would shoot you instantly."

"We're being 'held up' then?" I queried.

"Yes; that's it," he answered shortly.

At once all thought of my packet went out of my mind; I thought only of Dolores. I rose from my seat and, despite St. Nivel's remonstrance, passed rapidly to the rear of the brilliantly lighted train. I had met her as she came out of the dining-car, and she had told me she intended sitting with her aunt until it was time to retire for the night at ten o'clock. She intended to slip out, dear girl, for a few minutes before she went to bed to say good-night to me.

Now I found both her and her aunt in a great state of alarm.

"It's nothing serious, is it, Mr. Anstruther?" asked the elder lady, seizing my arm. "Some one here says that we are attacked by robbers."

Before I could answer, a man wearing a cowboy's high-crowned hat and a mask across the upper part of his face, appeared at the door of the car and gave the command –

"Hands up!"

He carried a revolver pointed upwards over his shoulder in such a position that he could have brought it down at once. At first I refused to elevate my hands as a fat Brazilian was doing near me, and this evoked another word of command –

"Hands up! Sharp!"

"*Do* put your hands up, dear," came the soft trembling voice of Dolores; "*do*, to please *me*."

My two hands shot up most willingly, immediately.

"Ladies," the man proceeded, in far from a disagreeable voice, "you have no need to fear. Our chief has fined each first-class passenger a hundred dollars; second-class passengers fifty dollars. If those amounts are placed on the seats, our collector will be round in a minute or two to take them up, then you will be at liberty to proceed."

At that moment another man, similarly attired, armed, and masked, joined the other at the door.

"He's in here," he announced. "That's him, no doubt."

He added a sentence in Spanish which I could not understand, then turned to me.

"Mr. William Anstruther?" he asked.

Involuntarily I answered him –

"Yes; my name is Anstruther."

"Follow me," he said sharply; "you're wanted."

I gave one look at Dolores, and she answered my look.

"You had better go with them, William," she said, calling me by my name for the first time. "I will come too."

She looked deadly white, and I feared every moment would faint.

The man who had entered first spoke again, addressing Dolores.

"You need not be afraid," he said. "We shall not harm Mr. Anstruther; and you had better remain where you are, because we shall probably have to *strip* him."

The two men laughed heartily at their coarse

joke, and I felt as if I could have killed them both.

Then the thought came unpleasantly home to me.

"*Why* would they want to strip me?"

I followed the first man down the corridor, and looking round saw the other standing at the door of the compartment in which I had left the ladies. He had a revolver in his hand, and was watching me intently. Had I made the slightest effort to escape, I have little doubt he would have shot me at once. My conductor took me back into the smoking-car, and then politely asked Lady Ethel, who was still there, to retire.

When she had gone, with wide-open eyes full of fear, fixed on me to the last glance, the masked man, who had me in charge, turned to me and made the following request: –

"Mr. Anstruther," he said, speaking in very good English, although one could tell it was not his native tongue, "we have reason to believe that you have concealed either on your person, or in your luggage, a certain packet which you are carrying to Valoro. Our chief requires that you shall give that packet up to him. That done, and your fine of a hundred dollars paid, you will be permitted to go on your way."

"And if I refuse to comply with your request?" I asked.

The man shrugged his shoulders.

"The chief will be here directly," he answered,

with a peculiar smile; "he will tell you himself."

I threw myself in a corner of the carriage, and with the bitterest thoughts at my heart, tried to think of some means of escape, while I awaited the coming of the principal brigand. St. Nivel sat opposite to me, and I saw by his set jaw and knitted brows that he considered the situation very serious. We had not long to wait for the chief. A heavy footstep came along the corridor and presently an immense bulk entered the doorway with a great masked head above it.

The man was a half-breed and a giant, possessing immense strength; the reason of his chieftainship was very evident.

"Which is Anstruther?" he asked abruptly, as he came in, with a strong foreign accent.

His subordinate pointed to me.

"*Carajo!* Mr. Anstruther," the giant began, "I hope you are not going to give us any trouble. You don't look very amiable!"

I simply looked at him and did not answer.

"My lieutenant here," the chief proceeded, "has no doubt acquainted you with my wishes. We want that little packet of yours, which you are carrying to Valoro."

"What little packet?" I asked superciliously.

"The little packet which you fetched from your lawyer's office just before you left London," he replied, with a smile; adding at my look of astonishment, "you see we know your movements pretty well."

I gave an impatient toss of my head, and felt inclined to drive my fist into the man's great fat face, the only part of which I could see was a great thick-lipped mouth with fine white teeth grinning through a black beard.

"Supposing," I said, "that I refuse to comply with your demand?"

"Then," he said abruptly, "we shall look for it." "Come now, Mr. Anstruther," he added, "we have very little time to lose; give me that packet."

"I haven't got it," I answered truthfully, for it was in St. Nivel's cigar-box.

The big man turned to his lieutenant.

"Send in a couple of the others; strip and search him," he said sharply.

In obedience to a call from the other, two more of the gang, big strong fellows, came in, and I prepared for a strong resistance.

Before, however, the men touched me, Sir Rupert Frampton's face appeared in the doorway; he had evidently just got out of bed, and wore a dressing-gown.

"It is no use whatever making any resistance to these men, Mr. Anstruther," he said, speaking in French; "you will probably lose your life if you do. Submit to what they demand, and we will make a claim against the Government at Valoro for whatever you lose. During the whole of my long connection with Aquazilia," he added, "I have only known such a robbery as this occur twice, and knowing the present peaceful and law-abiding state of the country, I cannot understand it."

"Very well then, Sir Rupert," I said, after a pause, "I will submit to these men, but I call upon you to witness my protest at the outrage!"

He nodded his head at my words, and in obedience to a further request from the giant, I proceeded to undress.

When this was done, they were not satisfied to search my clothes only, but took them away with them for further examination.

After returning me my light silk under-vest and drawers, they brought me a loose cowboy's dress, such as they wore themselves, and intimated that I must put it on.

It was no use demurring, so with a plaintive look at Sir Rupert, who, hardly able to repress his laughter, was still standing by, I did as I was bid.

"Now," proceeded the chief, "we have not found what we want about your person, Mr. Anstruther; we must look for it among your luggage."

He dangled my bunch of keys in his hand as he spoke. "Follow me, please."

The others closed round me and we went together to the luggage-car; here my luggage, which was fully marked with my name, was already set aside. They proceeded at once to thoroughly search each trunk, but replacing every article as they did so; loot was evidently not their object.

They came at last to the end of it; and the chief turned to me savagely.

"*Carajo!* Mr. Anstruther," he said, "you are playing with us. Do you refuse to tell us where this packet is?"

"Supposing I don't know?" I replied prevaricatingly, "supposing it is out of my power to tell you?"

"Then," he answered, with a savage oath, "we shall take you with us, and perhaps another besides, and hold you both as hostages until the packet is given up to us by *somebody*."

After a pause I shrugged my shoulders.

"You must do as you like," I said.

"Carlo," cried the chief at once, "see the fines are collected, and we will be off and take him with us."

"Who shall the other hostage be?" asked the lieutenant.

The big man stooped down and whispered in his ear.

The other man nodded and smiled in response to the other's laugh, but it appeared to me that he by no means relished the information conveyed to him in the whisper.

"Now, Mr. Anstruther," remarked the big half-breed, "we must trouble you to come with us, and don't take longer than you can help to say good-bye to the ladies."

This was intended by way of a joke; one which I did not appreciate.

"As soon as my cashier has been round collecting the dues," proceeded the big man, "we must be off. Don't you think you will change your mind, Mr. Anstruther, and give me that packet? If I had my way I would search the whole train for it, but we haven't got time, so we must take you instead."

St. Nivel looked up from his corner where he had sat, his hat drawn over his eyes.

"Have a cigar, Señor Capitano," he remarked to the chief, "while your man collects the cash. I've paid already."

He handed the man the box of cigars in which the packet was hidden. I thought it an act of madness.

"Thank you, Señor," replied the man, taking two; "a fine brand of cigars."

"Yes," replied my cousin, "they are very decent."

The Capitano took the box in his hands and smelt them.

"Yes, very nice," he remarked. "As good as anything you will get in Aquazilia."

Then St. Nivel did something which appeared to me to be an additional sign that he had taken leave of his senses.

"Won't you take the box, Capitano?" he asked.

The man smiled and shook his great head.

"Thank you," he said, "they are too mild for me."

St. Nivel shut the box up with what I thought was impatience, and threw it in the rack.

The thieves' cashier made his appearance with a bag full of dollars; then they all made a move for the door, taking me with them.

As we reached the platform of the smoking-car, and I was perforce about to jump down on to the permanent way, I saw the face of my servant Brooks looking up at me from the line.

"Let me give you a hand, sir," he said, with an expressive look in his eyes; "the ground's a bit rough here."

As he assisted me down in the darkness I felt him slip something under the loose cowboy's frock I wore and nudge me to take it; as I put my hand down, to my joy I felt it was my Colt's revolver!

I hastily thrust it into the belt under my smock-frock, where it was quite hidden.

Then the horses were brought round and we prepared to mount; but before we departed there was still a little ceremony to be gone through.

There were some left with drawn revolvers at the end of each carriage, almost to the last moment, but as the bulk of the band left the train they brought with them a half-breed dressed in the ordinary frock-coat and tall hat of civilisation, in a state of abject terror.

"Who is this man?" I asked the lieutenant, who happened to be near me.

He laughed as he twisted up a cigarette and answered me.

"He used to belong to our little society once," he said; "but he ran away and gave evidence against another member, who was shot."

"What are you going to do with him?" I asked.

He made a motion with his hand in his loose neckerchief of a man being hanged.

"No, surely not!" I cried, in horror.

"You'll see," he replied, as he began to smoke.

They dragged forward the shivering wretch, who had a prosperous look about him; and as they pulled him out of the train his tall hat fell off and rattled on the iron rails. No one stopped to pick it up; it was not worth while.

The man immediately following him carried his lasso in his hand. They lost very little time; there was a tree with a convenient branch, just near the line, and in a trice they threw the rope over this and knotted the end into a noose.

Then there was a call for a priest, and there happening to be a Padré in the train, the wretched man was accorded five minutes with him as he stood.

Within three minutes more the body of the half-breed was swinging and struggling in the air; but the struggles were not for long.

The desperadoes all around me whipped out their revolvers and commenced a rattling fusillade, the mark being the body of the man swinging on the tree.

* * * * *

My blood ran cold as I listened to the pinging of the bullets and the resounding shrieks of the ladies in the train.

Not till then did the last of the men leave the train, and one of them I saw, to my astonishment, bore in his arms apparently a woman in a cloak.

In a brilliant gleam of electric light, shot from the train in the darkness, I thought I saw the face of my Dolores, with a white gag across the mouth, but the idea seemed so preposterous that I did not give it another thought, thinking it to be some phantom of an overwrought brain, and the woman some light-o'-love of the desperado.

The man went straight to a horse, placed the burden he was carrying across the saddle-bow, sprang on to the horse, and with a number of others round him, including the chief, rode away.

They brought a horse for me and I mounted too, and rode along very unwillingly towards the end of the train. As we passed the engine, I saw that the fire-box had been raked out and water poured on it. There was a dense steam arising from it. I conjectured, and conjectured correctly, that they had done this to prevent the train steaming away and giving the alarm, for there was a considerable town not five miles off, the inhabitants of which were no doubt anxiously expecting the express.

When we arrived at the other side of the train, and the leading files of the robbers were passing off the railway line, the identity of the figure carried away across the saddle was put beyond all doubt, and the revelation nearly sent me mad.

Mrs. Darbyshire came shrieking out into the forepart of the car in which I had left her with Dolores.

"They have taken her," she shrieked, "they have taken her away from me as a hostage. It cannot be. Bring her back, bring her back, I implore you!" she cried in Spanish to the men who were passing the train, and who in return only laughed and jeered her.

"Mr. Anstruther," she cried, "save her!"

I made her no answer, for I knew it was useless, but I gripped the revolver I carried beneath my loose smock.

A great calmness came upon me then, though the blood surged through my head. Life was as nothing to me, compared with saving her; without her it would be worthless. I determined to use every art I was capable of, every ingenuity to outwit these ruffians and murderers, for her sake.

I began to laugh and talk with the men around me, at the same time noting every feature of the country as we left the railway behind and took a rough road.

As we emerged upon this, the moon rose and I could see that the road wound away in front of us, down into a valley where there was a thick wood and up the other side to great hills which were probably our destination. About two hundred yards in front of us rode the party who had carried off Dolores. To my great joy my party commenced to trot, and within ten minutes had caught up the party in front.

There was a good deal of talking in Spanish, which I did not understand. My eyes were fixed on the figure wrapped in the black cloak and lying across the saddle-bow of one of the ruffians.

As far as I could see, she was perfectly inanimate, but one thing I noticed, and that was the man who held her, a great, swarthy, black-bearded wretch, masked like the others, rode some six paces in rear of the rest.

This was sufficient for me; my plan was formed at once.

As we rode forward again, I felt that I had a good horse under me, and this was a satisfaction for the task I had in view. As we reached the wood at the foot of the hill, there were, I found to my great satisfaction, but two of the gang riding behind me and one by my side; the rest were in front. I had made myself agreeable, and rode so easily with them that the men around me had taken no special precautions to secure me; believing me to be unarmed, they evidently thought that I was powerless under the muzzles of their numerous revolvers.

They were mistaken.

As we plunged into the blackness of the road through the wood, I waited until we were well into it, then drew my revolver and shot the man riding on my right.

In the very act of firing, I dug the heels of my boots into my horse and caused him to swerve round.

Before they could draw, I shot both the men behind me, and as I tore past them, grasped the mask from the face of one as he fell. The whole thing was done in under ten seconds. I flew off like an arrow back towards the party we had just left, followed by a spattering fire from the men. I had left when they fully realised what had happened in the darkness.

I hastily fixed the black crape mask across my face as I cleared the wood, and made full gallop for Dolores.

As I came in sight of the party, they were evidently in alarm at the shooting, but I waved my arm to them assuringly and slowed down to a canter as I came near. They plainly regarded me from my mask as one of the gang.

I noticed to my satisfaction as I approached that the man in charge of Dolores was still some distance in the rear.

The road being narrow, and the men riding two abreast in it, I left the track and rode out into the rough ground as if I wished to reach the chief, crying out "Capitano!" as I passed the leading men, that being about all the Spanish I knew.

The great burly chief rode out as I approached, with a querulous look on his face as I saw it in the moonlight, as if he were annoyed, but the expression changed immediately, for I shot him through the body from my revolver as I held it concealed beneath the smock I wore; then I dashed for Dolores. I had still two chambers undischarged, and one of these I intended for the man bearing Dolores, but he was too quick for me; he turned his horse and bolted back along the road we had come and I after him. He was apparently in a panic. I roared out to him with all my might that if he would give up the lady I would spare his life, or otherwise he would be a dead man.

This hint seemed sufficient for him, for he slid off his horse and rolled away somewhere into the rough ground at the side of the road, leaving Dolores on the horse.

Then I saw that she had been secured to the high pommel of the Spanish saddle by a turn or two of a lasso.

We had gone fully three hundred yards more before I caught the horse which galloped away at full speed. Perhaps it was as well things happened thus, as the robbers were thundering behind, and had I taken the two burdens on one horse, we should I think, without doubt, have been recaptured. As it was, I lashed both horses to their fullest speed when I saw Dolores was secure, though evidently in great discomfort, yet it was a matter of life or death or worse.

Presently we came in view of the train getting up steam, though it was some distance off, and then a sight burst upon my view in addition which filled me with both joy and astonishment. About ten bicycles ridden by men were coming along the road, the slender spokes of their wheels glinting in the moonlight. They no sooner saw us than they raised a great shout, and waved their arms; it was then to my great thankfulness I saw the leading cyclist was my cousin, St. Nivel. I felt as if a ton weight of care had been lifted off my shoulders.

They made way for us as we came, and St. Nivel shouted to me as we passed through –

"Make straight for the train!"

I did as he bid me, and within five minutes had the pleasure of tearing the handkerchief with which she was gagged from my darling's mouth; and before all the assembled passengers kissing her upon the lips as I gave her insensible into the arms of her aunt.

I think I had earned those kisses!

Chapter XIII. Don Juan D'Alta

No sooner had we passed through the cyclists than they formed across the road and, dismounting, took up positions behind any cover which they discovered in the rough ground.

To my astonishment they unstrapped rifles from their machines, and as soon as the robbers appeared in pursuit greeted them with a rapid fire evidently from magazines. I saw several saddles emptied as they turned and rode off.

A few minutes after St. Nivel and his friends rejoined us.

"That was a lucky thought of mine," he said, laughing, when he had gripped my hand and congratulated me on our escape.

I remembered seeing the bicycles being put into the train at Monte Video, and the magazine rifles of course were in the guard's van, and ought to have been used when the robbers attacked us, but they came too suddenly and there was no time to get them.

From that time forward things went easily enough; steam was soon up, and we were away again to Valoro within half an hour. At the next station a special restaurant car was attached; we were treated like heroes, sitting amid the popping of champagne corks relating our adventures, and this went on long after the morning had broken.

But I, tired out, soon sought my bed in the sleeping-car, but not before I had been assured at the door of the ladies' car, by Mrs. Darbyshire, now all tears and smiles, that Dolores had regained consciousness, and was unhurt, save for bruises and, of course, a severe shock.

I slept until within an hour of our running into Valoro station late in the afternoon, and just had time to have a delicious bath and emerge fresh and hungry into the restaurant car in which St. Nivel, Lady Ethel, and Dolores looking very pale and ill, were just finishing lunch. My darling sat beside me while I lunched and held my hand – when it was disengaged – unheeded by Mrs. Darbyshire. This lady, I think, considered that the case had got beyond her and had better be relegated to a higher court – Don Juan d'Alta – for judgment.

Dolores even lighted my cigarette for me, but soon after her aunt took her away to prepare to leave the train.

"What on earth made you hand that poor devil of a brigand chief that box of cigars, Jack?" I asked St. Nivel, when we were alone with Ethel, and he had restored my precious casket to me; "he might have taken it and got the whole shoot."

"At that moment," replied St. Nivel, glancing through the rings of his cigar smoke quite affectionately at me, "I wished he *would* take it. Things looked very ugly for you, and we were powerless to help you. I thought if he took the cigar case the casket would at least be with you and you would know it and could use your own discretion about giving them the tip if your life were threatened as I imagined it would be."

"Very clever of you, Jack," I answered, "and I'm very much obliged to you for thinking of it, but I am glad that the poor devil didn't take it after all. I believe it to be my duty to take it to Don Juan d'Alta, even at the risk of my life."

St. Nivel sat thinking a moment or two; then he spoke.

"Why do you use the term 'poor devil'?" he asked, "when you speak of the robber chief?"

I told him why. I told him how I had shot him.

"Well, really, Bill," he said very seriously, "I wish the thing *had* gone. It has already cost several lives, and seems to carry ill-luck with it. Who knows how many more lives may be sacrificed? Of course, there cannot be a doubt but that the train was held up solely to obtain it; the taking of the hundred dollars a head was simply a ruse to cover the other. Old Frampton says such a raid on a train is a thing unheard of now in Aquazilia."

"Yes," I answered, "but it came to a good round sum all the same. Well, at any rate," I continued, as the train ran into Valoro station, "we've brought the thing to its destination, and we're all safe and sound, so there's *something* to be thankful for!"

At Valoro, things were "all right" as my man Brooks put it; news of the attack on the train, in which was the British Minister, had reached the capital, and a troop of cavalry awaited to escort him to his Legation.

"As I understand you have something of importance to deliver in Valoro," said Sir Rupert Frampton to me as we left the train, "I think you had better come in my carriage. I am taking Mrs. Darbyshire and the Señorita with me too. They both want reassuring, and the morale of the escort will do that. I shall take them right home."

"Thank you very much," I answered, "that will suit me down to the ground. My mission is to deliver a packet to Don Juan d'Alta himself."

"Then come along," added Sir Rupert, "for, of course, the ladies are going there too."

In a few minutes we were driving out of the station yard in a fine carriage, surrounded by soldiers.

It was the first time I had ever ridden with an escort, and I liked it.

We left the immense terminus, which would not have disgraced the finest city in Europe, and turned up a great boulevard leading to the higher part of the city where amid trees we could see many fine white houses.

"That is our house!" cried Dolores, as we left the houses behind and came out into the country. "Look, aunt! look, William!"

I did look and saw on the crest of the hill we were approaching, far away to the left, a long range of white buildings, relieved with towers, which looked like a small castle.

It filled me with apprehension, for it was a sign of the great wealth of her father – the wealth which I feared would be a bar to our union.

I think she was surprised at the glum look on my face for the rest of the little journey.

"Are you sorry to go and see my father?" she asked plaintively, with a sweet look in her blue eyes. "I am sure he will be very glad to see *you* and to thank you for saving me. He is a very kind man is my father," she added solemnly, "very kind to me, and very kind to his reptiles."

Before them all – Mrs. Darbyshire was now quite resigned – I took her hand and pressed it.

"It is a very easy thing to be kind to *you*, Dolores," I said. "I should find the difficulty in being kind to the reptiles."

"But you will humour my father, won't you?" she asked, and then dropped her voice, "for both our sakes?"

The amount of interest dear old Sir Rupert Frampton took in distant scenery during this drive, and the many objects of interest he pointed out to Mrs. Darbyshire to divert her attention from us, made me his willing slave for life. For, indeed, I was agitated at the prospect of the interview which was to come in a few minutes with old Don Juan d'Alta, not only for our sake, but for the sake of the dear old lady at Bath, who I doubted not was now dead, and the packet she had confided to my care.

It was a comfort to sit with Dolores' little hand in mine. My other clasped the precious packet in my trousers pocket.

At last we drove into a great avenue filled with

the most luxuriant tropical vegetation, very carefully tended, for there were men at work everywhere.

The escort wheeled away into line as we swept under a great glass-roofed portiere, and came to a halt at a fine flight of marble steps, where Sir Rupert left us and drove away with the soldiers clattering around him.

Yes, the home of my Dolores was like a modern palace.

Overcome with seeing it again, I think she forgot even me for the moment. She ran gaily up the steps, trilling with laughter.

"Where is father?" she cried.

That gentleman answered her question in person.

At the head of the steps appeared an old man dressed in black with an abundance of perfectly white hair which surrounded a very good-humoured, wrinkled face, almost as brown as a berry. It was the face of an aristocrat, but of an aristocrat who lived in the open air, and a good deal under the burning sun of an Aquazilian summer.

He came forward with a very loving smile on his old face and took his little daughter in his arms.

Their greeting was in Spanish and therefore most of it was lost to me, but I took it to be a very affectionate one. This over, the conversation turned in my direction and broke into English.

"This is the gentleman who saved me from the

robbers, father," exclaimed Dolores; "this is Mr. William Anstruther."

The old man turned towards me with extended hands, his face beaming.

"Mr. Anstruther," he said, speaking in very fair English, which I found most of the gentry spoke there, "let me take your hands and thank you from my heart for your heroic conduct to my daughter. The news of the outrage and your gallant escape reached us together by telegraph the first thing this morning. Indeed, I think they had the news at the club last night."

When he had at last let my hand go, I got in a word of my own.

"Naturally," I began, "you will like to spend some time with your daughter, but when you are at liberty I have an important message to deliver to you."

"Indeed!" he said, looking rather surprised. "From whom?"

"From an old lady who formerly lived at Bath, in England," I replied, "but who now, I fear, is dead – murdered!"

"Good heavens!" he cried; "who can it be?"

"It was a lady known by the name of Carlotta Altenberg," I answered.

"Good God!" he cried, throwing up his hands excitedly; "poor old d'Altenberg murdered!"

I was rather disappointed at his tone. It was

very certain that the old lady was a person of little importance, or he would never have spoken of her like that.

In a moment or two he turned to me again.

"I have taken the liberty," he said, "of having your luggage and that of your friends with whom you are travelling – and whom Dolores tells me are your cousins – brought up here. I could not think of allowing you to stay anywhere else in Valoro than under my roof, and I am vain enough to think that we can keep you amused during your stay."

I made suitable acknowledgments for his kindness, and was wondering all the while, in my heart, under what lucky star I had been born to be located beneath the very roof with my Dolores, and that, too, at her father's invitation. But he broke in upon my thanks.

"Not another word, Mr. Anstruther," he said; "it is you who confer the benefit upon me.

"Now, you say you have a message from the poor old Baroness d'Altenberg for me. Good! I will show you to my study, and there we will go into the matter at our leisure."

He led me down a long corridor to a beautiful room overlooking the valley, communicating with a long range of what looked like conservatories. Hardly necessary, I thought, in such a climate!

"Now," said my host, placing a box of cigars before me, "amuse yourself with these, and my servant shall bring us some champagne to celebrate your arrival. I will just go and see my sister and little Dolores settled in their apartments, then I will come back to you and we can have our talk. You shall tell me all about the poor Baroness."

The kind old man pressed me down into a comfortable lounge chair, then with a smile departed.

I took a good look round the room, and took stock of its contents. It was furnished very luxuriously in the European fashion and contained some beautiful pictures, but its principal ornaments were cases of stuffed reptiles of every sort, from a tiny lizard to a great boa-constrictor with red jaws agape.

There were four French windows opening to the ground, shaded by outside striped blinds similar to those used in England, but not low enough to hide a most splendid view of hill and dale and far-away mountains, which seemed to surround the city of Valoro, itself seeming to rest on a plateau.

I was standing looking at a case of particularly objectionable yellow snakes when I heard one of the French windows move behind me; turning, I came face to face with the polite lieutenant of the band of robbers who had attacked our train. He had discarded the cowboys' dress and wore the clothes of a gentleman. He at once raised a revolver to the level of my head as I started back, and addressed me in perfectly polite tones.

"Come, come, Mr. Anstruther," he said, "it's no good. I want that packet. If you don't give it to me I shall simply shoot you through the head and take it."

It appeared to me that my journey after all had

been in vain; there was the muzzle of the pistol within six inches of my head, and I had to make up my mind about it.

St. Nivel's words came back to me concerning the ill-luck of it, and I could almost hear him saying –

"Let the thing go; it isn't worth risking your life for."

Then I thought of Dolores, and on this thought broke the voice of the robber, cold and hard.

"You must make up your mind, Mr. Anstruther," he said, "while I count ten, otherwise I must fire."

He commenced counting slowly.

"One."

The thought of Dolores grew stronger.

"Two."

I could almost *hear* St. Nivel's voice urging me to give it up.

"Three."

Then there was my promise to the old lady, murdered, I believed, by these infamous ruffians. I hesitated.

"Four."

"Five."

"Six."

Then came another thought: would the old lady, who had been spoken of as the Baroness d'Altenberg, hold me to my word under the circumstances?

"Seven."

"Eight."

I doubted it.

"Nine."

I had made up my mind to save my life for Dolores.

"Hold," I said; "I will give it to you!"

He smiled.

"I think you are very sensible," he said; "anybody else but an Englishman would have given it up long ago, and then a great deal of trouble and several lives would have been saved."

I put my hand in my pocket despising myself the while for giving way, but still convinced that I should have been a fool to throw my life away under the circumstances.

"Perhaps you will tell me," I asked, as I drew the packet from my pocket, "how it is that you know I am here and that I have the packet with me?"

He laughed.

"I may as well tell you," he said, "that you have never been left unwatched since you left Bath."

"You seem to know my movements pretty well

yourself," I said, in an astonished tone.

"Pretty well," he answered, with another smile.

I had no sooner drawn the packet from my pocket than he snatched it unceremoniously from my hands and walked with it towards the window.

"Don't move," he cried to me, "until I tell you *or* I shall fire. I must verify the contents before I leave you."

He still held the pistol in my direction and I have no doubt would have fired had I made the slightest move towards him, which I could not have done without making some noise, for about six paces divided us.

I stood still and regarded him as he tore off the covering with his teeth.

He was so thoroughly engrossed with the task that he did not hear a slight rustling sound which caused me to turn my head towards the door which led to the long range of what appeared to be glass houses, and which was just open a little. What I saw there made me turn cold from head to foot.

Gliding through the slightly open door, and pushing it farther open as it came with its immense bulk, was a huge black and yellow snake!

It was moving in the direction of the robber, who, entirely engrossed with the packet from which he had torn the wrapper, was totally oblivious of his position. The snake had possibly been attracted by the tearing noise which he had made as he rent the linen envelope with his teeth.

I had almost cried aloud to warn him, when, I checked myself. The man had come to murder me; he must take his chance. He had turned to me, satisfied with his scrutiny of the casket which he now held in his hand, the box which contained it having been thrown on the floor, when I saw the snake draw itself into a great coil and raise its head; then, just as his lips were opening to speak to me, the great reptile made a spring, and in an instant coiled itself tight round him, the tail whipping close like a steel wire. He gave a great cry and dropped the casket and the revolver immediately. Within a second or two I had them in my hands, and at the same moment the door opened and Don Juan d'Alta entered.

He rapped out a great Spanish oath, and a good many more words in the same language; then he turned to me.

"Who is this man?" he asked.

"That is one of the men," I answered at once, "who attacked the train. He entered this room a few minutes after you left me with the intention of robbing or murdering me."

"Then he seems to have got his deserts," replied my host, laughing. He came quite close to me and whispered in my ear, "The snake is quite harmless, but it will give him a fright and maybe break a rib or two if it squeezes hard."

The old man appeared to regard it as a huge joke, but kept a solemn face.

It appeared to be going beyond a joke to break

his ribs, and I said so in a whisper.

"He deserves it," was the reply.

Meanwhile, the robber was becoming absolutely livid with fear, and began to supplicate Don Juan in Spanish.

Finding this of no avail, he turned to me.

"Have mercy, Señor," he cried piteously, "and help me to free myself from this reptile. It is crushing me to death."

The horrible thing with wide-open jaws was breathing in his face, and its fetid breath seemed turning him sick.

Don Juan laughed aloud, rather heartlessly it seemed to me, but the Spanish nature is a cruel one to its enemies.

"I know the man," he said, "and I cannot understand what has brought him into this *galère*. Let us question him?"

* * * * *

I could not quite see that a man enveloped in the embrace of a boa-constrictor, even though the reptile might be tame and harmless, would be a person likely to give either correct or coherent answers to questions, but I acquiesced in Don Juan d'Alta's suggestion that we should try and get some information out of him.

He commenced at once; speaking in English for my benefit.

"What induced you and your band to attack the train yesterday?" was his first question.

"I don't know," was the answer.

"That is a lie," responded Don Juan, speaking quite coolly. "If you wish to get out of the coils of that snake, you must speak the truth.

"Now come, I know of course who you are, I know everybody in Valoro, and especially the members of the Carlotta Society, which is avowedly Royalist and opposed to the present Government like myself. You are a member of that Society; you are one of its leaders. I suggest to you that the so-called band of robbers who attacked the train last night were simply members of the Carlotta Society?"

"I admit," gasped the man, trying with all his force to keep the boa-constrictor's head away from his face, "that I am a leader of the Carlotta Society, but I cannot disclose its secrets even to you."

"You must speak, Lopes," Don Juan said, "or you will not get free. Remember that I am a member of the Carlotta Society myself, though an honorary one on account of my age. You will never get back to your desk in the bank of Valoro if you don't speak."

"It is inhuman!" cried the man desperately, "it is vile torture!"

"It is also inhuman," added Don Juan sententiously, "to raid trains, and to threaten murder as you have done in this room. Your band too was none too scrupulous in hanging Jimenez the half-breed, though he was an informer. Tell me now, why did you hold up the train? why did you try to rob this English gentleman?"

"It was done," answered the man stertorously, for he was becoming weak, "it was done on urgent orders from Europe from our head."

Don Juan started, and going close whispered a name in his ear.

"Yes," replied Lopes faintly, but I heard the words, "from the Duke himself."

As Don Juan turned from him with a perplexed look, his eye caught the casket which I still held in my hand; he lost colour and became very agitated as he saw it.

"Where did you get that from?" he asked abruptly, seizing my hand.

I opened my hand and placed the casket in his.

"From the Baroness d'Altenberg," I replied. "I made the journey from Europe to give it to you. My task is accomplished."

The casket had reached its destination.

Chapter XIV. The Casket

"Now there are two favours I wish to ask you, Don Juan," I said, as he stood with the precious casket in his hands, "the first is to put that casket in a place of safety; the second to release this poor wretch from the snake."

He awoke from a fit of deep meditation with a start.

"I will grant your two favours immediately," he answered quickly as he put the casket in his breast pocket and buttoned his frock-coat over it; "see one is already done, now I will accomplish the other."

He went to the end of the apartment, and lifting a curtain hanging over the base of a bookcase, took from a shelf there a silver bowl, filled apparently with bread and milk.

With this he went out on to the terrace, through the French windows, and commenced to make a peculiar sibilant noise between his teeth, half whistle half hiss.

It had a most peculiar effect upon the boa-constrictor, who, from the first production of the silver bowl, had shown a lively interest in it by moving its great head up and down excitedly. The noise made by Don Juan, however, decided it; it began to uncoil itself from the would-be assassin and finally dropped on the floor with a "slump" and wriggled out of the window on to the terrace. As the man was released, I covered him with the revolver as I was taking no risks, but it was quite unnecessary, as he fell fainting on a couch to which he had staggered almost immediately he was free.

Don Juan returned from the terrace with a pleased smile.

"My pets are a great source of comfort to me," he remarked as he sank into a chair, after courteously making me take another. "To see that poor dumb thing take its food so healthily compensates me almost for the shock which this villainous fellow has given us."

"Snakes," he continued, "are greatly affected by sound, as no doubt you noticed just now. There is little question that the snake was attracted to Lopes by some sound."

"But still," he continued, placing his hand in his breast, "the sight of the casket which you have brought to me is a greater shock than the desperado's pistol presented at your head was to you."

He passed his hand over his forehead as if the idea bewildered him.

"And you say you got it from the Baroness d'Altenberg?" he asked.

"Yes," I answered, "I took it from the safe at her direction."

"Whatever can it contain?" he muttered to himself; then the figure of Lopes lying on the sofa caught his eye.

"We must have this fellow removed," he said. "What shall we do with him?"

I looked at the recumbent figure for some time, and it only inspired me with pity.

"I think he ought to be sent somewhere," I proposed, "where he would be taken care of and prevented from doing further mischief. Have you a hospital in Valoro?"

The old gentleman looked at me in some surprise.

"I assure you," he answered, "that we have two, as fine as any in Europe."

"Then," I said, "if I may make the suggestion, I would have Lopes sent off to one."

Don Juan rang the bell immediately, and when a servant answered it, he indicated the man on the couch and gave some order in Spanish to him.

"They will take him away," he explained, "and send him down to the hospital in one of my carriages. There we can have him arrested later if it is worth while."

In a very short time two men appeared and carried Lopes out of the room.

Then we sat down facing one another, and Don Juan produced the casket from his pocket and stood contemplating it upon his knee.

"Whatever could have prompted the old Baroness d'Altenberg to send me this," he cogitated half to himself, "after so many years; and what can it contain?"

I made a suggestion.

"Supposing you open it," I said, "while I walk in the garden."

"My dear Mr. Anstruther," he said, quite frightened at giving me so much trouble, "that is not at all necessary. I can go into my little cabinet here."

He indicated a small room, the door of which stood partly open, and revealed a little study with a writing table and a reading lamp.

"If you will excuse me for five minutes," he added, "I will retire into that little room and open the casket!"

"But have you the keys?" I asked.

He nodded with a smile.

"Oh yes," he answered, "those three little locks and the secret of opening them are very familiar to me, but I have not seen it for a great many years."

I did not in the least understand what he was alluding to, but I, of course, urged him to retire into his little room and examine the contents of the casket in peace, while I amused myself in the study itself.

"You will find some marvellous stuffed specimens of the green lizard in those lower cases," he remarked, as he disappeared into his sanctum. "I should advise you to study them closely."

He had no sooner disappeared into the little room, the door of which he left slightly open, when I mentally consigned the green lizards and, in fact, the whole lacertilian family to a place warmer than the plains of Aquazilia in summer even, and sat idly wondering how long it would be before I saw Dolores again.

I distinctly heard the click of a lock as the old gentleman opened the ebony casket, there was a pause and a long silence broken only by the crackling of paper. Then I heard him give a cry of astonishment, and a Spanish exclamation it was – "Madre de Dios!"

An invocation only used on occasions of great excitement.

Then I heard a low muttering as he repeated certain passages, possibly of the letter, to himself, but it was in a foreign language, probably Spanish, and entirely unintelligible to me.

Another pause followed, then the door opened again and Don Juan re-entered the room, but his appearance had entirely changed.

His healthy sunburnt complexion had lost all its colour and was of a leaden hue, his eyes were starting from beneath his bushy eyebrows, and his right hand, as he laid it on the back of a chair, trembled like a leaf in the wind.

"Mr. Anstruther," he said with difficulty, "it will be necessary for me to leave for Europe as soon as possible, for England, for Bath!"

If he had said that he had just made up his mind to go to the moon I could not have been more astonished!

"To England!" I repeated.

"Yes, to England, and that as soon as possible."

The whole thing seemed to me extremely curious.

"Forgive my asking the question," I said, "but do you mind telling me why you want to visit Bath?"

He considered for some moments, passing his hand across his forehead, which was clammy with perspiration.

"Before I answer that question," he said at last, "I should like to ask you another.

"I understand that you have met the lady who entrusted you with the casket which you have given me, at a certain house in a street called Monmouth Street in the town of Bath?"

"Yes, that is so," I answered.

"Are you aware that there was a safe in that house. A steel safe of peculiar workmanship?"

"Yes," I replied, "I have seen it and opened it. I told you so."

"Ah! then you can tell me," he cried excitedly, "what was in the safe?"

"I'm afraid I cannot; I opened the safe at the request of the old lady, who, at that time, was lying sorely wounded on her bed. I opened it hastily, took out what I was directed to take by a note within, then closed the safe again."

"But the safe was not empty?"

"No, I think I can go so far as to say that there

appeared, as well as I recollect from the hasty glance I had, to be other documents and parcels behind those which I took away."

"Very good," Don Juan replied; "now tell me something more. In whose charge is that house in the street of Monmouth. Do you happen to know?"

"When I left Bath," I replied, "the house was in charge of a sergeant of police and his wife; they were caretakers."

"Very good, very good indeed," answered the old man, apparently much relieved; "now tell me one thing more. When does the ship by which you came return to England?"

"The *Oceana* returns in about a fortnight's time."

"Do you think now, if I used my best endeavours to make that fortnight very agreeable to you, and to show you during that time more, perhaps, than you would see of Aquazilia in a month in the ordinary way, that I could induce you to return to England with me by that ship?"

At first I thought that by agreeing with his request I should be leaving Dolores behind, then I remembered that I could induce him perhaps to take her with him.

I hesitated for a time and he pressed me.

"Come, now, Mr. Anstruther," he said, "give me your answer."

"I am perfectly certain," I said hesitatingly, for I was not going to give myself away, "that you will make our stay delightful, but I think, before I answer, I had better let you into a little secret.

"I happen to know that my cousin, Lord St. Nivel, and his sister, Lady Ethel Vanborough, intend asking you and Donna Dolores to spend some time with them in England. Could you not make this visit answer both purposes?"

"That would necessitate my taking my daughter with me," he said rather dubiously; then a light seemed to break in upon him, and a smile hovered about his lips to which the colour was just returning.

"Should my daughter have no objection," he replied guardedly, "I see no reason why she should not accompany us."

I know my face lighted up with pleasure. I could not control it.

"We shall spend Christmas with you," I said cheerfully at last, "at any rate, and Christmas in Valoro will be a great novelty both to my cousins and myself, I have no doubt."

"Christmas and the New Year are the gayest times with us of the whole twelve months," he answered, "and you will be able to be present at them both."

"The prospect," I cried, "is delightful, and I will return with you, Don Juan, with pleasure. I should be most ungrateful to refuse your kind offer. I think I can answer for my cousins too, as they have really only taken this trip to please me."

"Very well, then," he said rising, "that's settled;

now we will go and find the ladies. I have no doubt your cousins have arrived by this time. I sent an automobile for them."

As I followed him, I flattered myself that I could persuade Dolores to take that return journey with us to Europe, if any persuasion were indeed necessary, by which it will be seen that I was acquiring a certain amount of confidence in my powers over that young lady.

Chapter XV. The Abbot of San Juan

The two weeks which followed constituted, I have no hesitation in saying, the gala fortnight of my existence.

I never could have imagined it possible that so much pleasure could have been crowded into such a short time. But can it not be easily believed that everything then was to me gilded with that supreme fine gold, the glamour of a young love? Yes, I think even the old Don himself saw it, and at any rate did not forbid it.

I went about with Dolores everywhere, even to church, at which she was a regular attendant, and I flatter myself behaved very creditably there, for though I was not a Roman Catholic like herself, yet I had attended the Sunday evening ministrations of the monks of Bath, and knew a good deal about it through the said monks' discourses.

I hope I don't make a mistake in calling them monks – if I do, I ask their pardon. I certainly understood them to *say* they were monks.

Be that as it may. I did not disgrace Dolores when I went with her to the great cathedral in Valoro.

But our time there was by no means entirely spent in going to church. Day after day the old Don engaged special trains in which we flew about the Republic faring sumptuously everywhere, and on our return there would generally be a dinner-party, followed by the theatre or the opera – a magnificent house and performance – and as likely as not a ball after that. Much more of it would have killed us all.

But the gay life mercifully drew towards a close, and Dolores and I began to contemplate a pleasurable voyage back on that very ship on which we had first met and loved.

Yes, loved; we were plighted lovers now; there was no secret, no hiding anything from one another.

By Dolores' wish I only waited to reach England to tell her father of my love for her and ask him for her.

"And do you think he will give you to me, darling?" I asked one beautiful night, when we were sitting out a waltz at a ball at the house of a grandee at Valoro. "Do you think he will give you to an Englishman?"

"Considering that he gave his sister away to an Englishman I don't see how he can refuse me to you, dearest," she answered. "At any rate I think I can persuade him."

Yes, I believed she could, she looked capable of persuading the angels themselves, in her dress of white silk, cut rather low, with a string of pearls round her neck worth about the value of the winner of the Derby.

Towards the last few days of our stay in Aquazilia, when we were all, even Lady Ethel, surfeited with dancing, and St. Nivel and I began to look askance at banquets, Don Juan came to me one day and took me aside into his garden.

I purposely led him away from the direction of the reptile houses of which I had a holy horror, and we sauntered down a shady avenue of palms.

"There is one place of interest near Valoro, Mr. Anstruther," he said, "which I should much like to show you and Lord St. Nivel if he cares to come, and that is the great Trappist Monastery at San Juan del Monte, about ten miles from here."

"By Jove!" I answered, "that is the very place I should like to see! I'm your man at any time."

"If you can be up by seven to-morrow morning," continued the old man, "we can motor over in the cool of the day. I know it is asking a good deal of you, because we have this evening to attend the reception of your minister, and then go on to the ball at Donna Elvira della Granja's. At the earliest we shall not be in bed till two, I fear."

"Never mind," I answered, "a cold tub usually puts me straight after a late night, and I am particularly anxious to see some real live monks in real cells."

"You will see both there in dozens," replied d'Alta; "there are nearly three hundred monks there."

Despite the dissipation of the night, six o'clock the next morning saw me out of bed, and 7.45 found me dressed for the road and as fresh from my cold bath as if His Britannic Majesty's Minister at Valoro had not given a reception at all, and Donna Elvira della Granja's ball had never taken place, though I certainly put in an appearance at the former, sitting in a corner with Dolores and listening to her description of all the political notabilities present, and at the latter I certainly did my duty as an Englishman, as many a black-eyed donna could testify, albeit I had all the best waltzes with Dolores, and of course took her in to supper.

I think every one in Valoro by this time put us down as an engaged couple; especially as old Don Juan seemed a consenting party or discreetly blind to our proceedings.

St. Nivel told me afterwards of a conversation he overheard between two American attachés at Donna Elvira's.

"I guess," remarked the "Military" to the "Naval," "that Englishman's goin' to walk off with old d'Alta's girl."

"You bet," confirmed the Naval, "he's fairly on the job. What is he?"

"Well, he's the cousin of that young Lord St. Nivel," responded the Military, "and that counts a lot, of course. But his *real* trade I'm told is book writing."

"Jeehosophat!" commented the Naval. "I guess he'll chuck that when he's Don Juan's son-in-law; the old snake-charmer will never tolerate a mere *bookman* in his drawing-room. His blue Spanish blood would all turn green, I reckon."

Thus was the humble calling of a novelist despised, even in Valoro!

When, however, I descended from my bedroom at 7.45, after partaking of a delicious *petit déjeuner* of coffee, milk, bread, and fruit in my apartment, I found Don Juan d'Alta ready for the road, and the motor at the door. In five minutes St. Nivel joined us.

"I didn't like to be left behind, old sportsman," he exclaimed. "Staying in bed on a huntin' mornin' is not exactly my form, even when the quarry is merely a harmless Trappist!"

"Your early habits do you credit, but your language, St. Nivel," I said reprovingly, "is verging on the profane."

"I'm sure I'm very sorry," he answered. "I'd walk ten miles rather than offend any one's feelings. I hope Don Juan didn't hear me."

"Don Juan is a man of the world," I answered, "and it wouldn't matter if he did, but other people might hear you and not like it."

"Righto, Bill," replied my sporting cousin. "I'll keep my eye on you and try and not put my foot in it."

In a few minutes we were rattling through some magnificent mountain scenery, with luxuriant vegetation and lovely wild flowers on every side. On the tops of the trees were parrots of varied colours which, disturbed by the noise of the motor, fluttered in all directions before us.

"Now I particularly want you to notice the abbot," said Don Juan as we approached the monastery, a very ancient-looking pile of buildings situated in a most lonely spot on the side of a mountain, yet surrounded by scenery which would have rivalled any in the world; "he is a most remarkable man, and possesses, as you will see, a most remarkable presence."

Presently we drew up at a very plain front door, and were immediately reconnoitred through a small wicket hole.

"The janitor," observed St. Nivel, "is evidently taking stock of us, and for that reason, Bill, I feel thankful that you have put on that new Norfolk suit; it gives the whole party a classy appearance."

The survey seemed satisfactory. Some bolts were shot back and the door opened, disclosing a monk in a brown habit.

He made some evidently most respectful remarks to Don Juan in Spanish, and then we all entered the monastery and were shown into a guest-room.

Here in a few minutes another lay brother brought a liqueur stand with glasses.

"Veritable Chartreuse," remarked Don Juan, as he laid his hand on the little decanters of green and yellow liquid, "the true stream drunk at the source!"

He filled the little glasses and handed them round as the lay brother stood looking on admiringly.

"You must take some," he said, "or they will be offended."

St. Nivel sipped his glass appreciatively.

"The monk who invented this," he remarked

sententiously, "*deserved* to go to heaven."

"Our abbot will give himself the honour of wait-ing upon your lordships," were the lay brother's parting words as translated to us by Don Juan.

We possessed our spirits in contentment, and awaited his coming, whilst d'Alta expatiated on the rigours of the Trappists' life, their isolation, their silence, their exactness in the keeping of the Office of the Church.

I fear this discourse, earnest though it was on the part of our host, was lost upon St. Nivel, whom I detected catching flies – and liberating them imme-diately – in the most solemn part. To him the sever-est form of penance was represented by a life from which all descriptions of "huntin'" and "shootin'" were excluded. He had been burning to kill some-thing big in the game line ever since he had set foot on shore, and I was quite prepared to hear him ask the abbot when he arrived whether he was "a huntin' man." He had asked that question of almost every-body we had met up to then in Aquazilia.

The abbot, however, came at last, just as Don Juan was concluding an account of St. Bruno, the Founder of the Order, and Jack was sitting with his eyes stolidly fixed upon the liqueur decanter.

Yes, the abbot was all d'Alta had said; he was a man of fifty, tall, spare, straight as a dart, but unlike most of the other monks we saw, fair and fresh col-oured.

I stood looking at him for some time, gazing into his fair open face, after he had taken my hand

and released it. I wondered who it was he reminded me of, whose face he brought so vividly to my recollection. Yet striking as the likeness was to *some one*, I could not recall who that some one was.

"You must be hungry after your drive, gentlemen," he said, speaking very fair English, as indeed most educated people did in Aquazilia. "I have ordered *déjeuner* at once for you. While it is preparing would you like to see the monastery?"

St. Nivel and I at once expressed our pleasure at the prospect, and the abbot preceded us, walking with Don Juan, but stopping occasionally to turn and speak to us and point out some object of interest.

In this way we passed through the wonderful institution and saw the Trappists each in his little abode, a sort of cottage to himself in which he ate and slept, and worked *alone*. At stated hours all through the day and night, the hundreds of monks met in the church to recite the office.

Don Juan told us as we stood on the steps of the great corridor that he had spent a week there in retreat before his marriage, and kept the "Hours" with the community.

Pointing down the corridor which stretched before us, he said the sight which struck him most was to stand as we did, on a night in winter and hear the great bell ring for Matins.

"Then," said he, "all those doors of the little houses open, and from each comes out a monk with a lantern. They look like hundreds of fireflies all going towards the great Abbey church."

I think the abbot saw with that intuitive knowledge which belongs to a refined nature that St. Nivel was *bored*; he steered us back to the guest-room, where a most excellent lunch was awaiting us – soup, fish, a dish of cutlets and a sweet omelette, all excellent, and served with red and white wine-like nectar and coffee from the Trappists' estate on the hills.

The abbot did not eat with us, but sat and charmed us with his conversation, for charming it was.

He talked with that fascinating fluency which one would have expected to find in a travelled man of the world rather that in a cloistered monk. He held us during all that meal, giving zest to each dish that came, with anecdotes of every country, and yet he spoke with a refined simplicity and perfect innocence of thought. His clear-cut and healthy face, his bright blue eyes and white teeth, the exceeding sweetness of his face and expression are with me now as I write.

When it was over and we had parted from him and were flying back to Valoro and modernism, I turned to Don Juan and spoke my thoughts.

"And where," I asked, "can the Order of Trappists have gained such a wonderful recruit from?"

The old man's face, which had been smiling, turned very grave; he shook his head and sighed.

"Ah! I wish I could tell you!"

That was his answer.

Chapter XVI. The Confession of Brooks

We left Valoro a few days after the great festival of the New Year, which came as a fitting finale to all our gaiety.

Christmas had been a quiet, sedate feast in the nature of a Sunday. We left just as the premonitory signs of the rainy season were making themselves apparent.

St. Nivel's friends, the American attachés, told him that we were well out of it, as the rains were torrential.

Dolores and I commenced the journey with much satisfaction; up to the last we had feared that Don Juan might have altered his mind and left his daughter at home, but I think the old gentleman began to understand, if he thought about it at all, that if he left Dolores behind, he would also have to leave me too.

Our departure was on the morrow of a great banquet, given by Don Juan to many of the notabilities of Valoro in our honour.

It was one of the grandest dinners I was ever present at, and the display of ladies' dresses and jewels would have done credit to a court function at home. But I think the sweet simple beauty of Dolores and my cousin Ethel took the palm. On this occasion I took in to dinner a grave and important donna with a distinct beard and moustache. I was told that she was a model of piety and that *all* – or nearly all – pious old ladies in Aquazilia had beards and moustaches!

Dolores sat opposite me on this occasion, and the way in which a young military attaché of Brazil paid her attention under my very nose, stamped him at once in my estimation, with his curled-up moustache, as a mere puppy!

I am sure Dolores thought so too, although she *did* listen to his trashy conversation, because when we were saying "good-night" – hastily under one of the big palms on the terrace – oh! if he could have seen us – she told me with her two dear arms round my neck that she only loved me, and I was not to look so *jealous* another time at a dinner-party, but talk to my partner whether she had a beard and moustache or not. Just as if I *could* look jealous and of *such* a man!

And so we left Aquazilia behind with its sunshine and lavish hospitality, and took ship again – the dear old *Oceana* – for our own foggy island, which I did not much relish returning to in February.

But Dolores was with me and she made sunshine everywhere.

We had been a fortnight on our return voyage, when an incident occurred which filled me with surprise and concern.

It was one of those grey days at sea when the prospect of the mingled ocean and sky is not very attractive.

St. Nivel was in the smoking-room; Dolores and Ethel were in the state-room of the latter, holding one of those long important feminine conferences – most delightful, I understood, to themselves – in which dress was the *pièce de résistance*, with perhaps a little gossip about Ethel's conquests in Aquazilia; they were legion! Mrs. Darbyshire was asleep in her state-room, and as for the dear old man, Don Juan, whom I looked upon now as my future father-in-law, he was studying assiduously a book he had picked up in the ship's library, *Reptiles of England, Scotland, and Wales*.

Simple soul! He might just as well have studied the snakes of Ireland for all he would see of them in England at that time of the year, unless he went to the Zoo, and then I understand he would not see much.

Our party being thus disposed of, I was sitting alone in a sheltered part of the promenade deck – for there was a bit of a wind – rather depressed at the dreary grey prospect I was contemplating. I was absolutely alone.

Perhaps I had been sitting thus half an hour, wrapped up in a Burberry, when I heard a soft foot-step approaching, and my man Brooks stood before me. I noticed that he too looked depressed, and I put his expression down too to the effect of the weather. He stood there for a moment in silence, then preferred a request.

"May I speak to you for a few minutes, sir?" he asked.

I straightened myself up in my deck chair, and took a good look at him; he certainly appeared very solemn, as if he had got something on his mind.

"Certainly, Brooks," I answered, "what's the matter?"

The man had been a most excellent servant, and indeed I considered I owed my life to him, and perhaps Dolores' as well, for had he not handed me my Colt's revolver on that memorable night when the train was attacked, and I was being carried off by the supposed robbers? He availed himself of his permission to speak very slowly; he appeared to be turning something over in his mind, and whatever it was, was apparently not very agreeable. He stood at "attention," the habit of an old soldier, with his forehead puckered; at last his lips opened, and he commenced what he had to say.

"When you engaged me, sir," he began, "you were under the impression that I was a straightforward English servant. Sir," he added, "I was nothing of the sort."

I looked at his bronzed, clean-shaven face, fair hair and soldier's blue eyes, in wonderment.

"What are you talking about, Brooks?" I asked. The man's tone disturbed me. I had grown quite fond of him, and feared he was going to give notice. He was a most perfect valet, the best by far that I had ever come across.

"You thought I was straight, sir," he continued, "and I wasn't. It was like this, sir: when I left the army I was taken as valet by the Dook of Birmingham; his brother had been an officer in my old regiment, and I had been his servant.

"I lived with the Dook over two year, and then when we were staying in a big house near Sandringham there was some jewellery of the Dook's missed, and His Grace told me that, although he made no charge against me, he should get another valet.

"I give you my word, sir, as I stand here, that I knew nothing of the missing jewellery. I was as innocent of stealing it as a babe unborn.

"But I knew perfectly well that the thing would stand against me, and that I should be a marked man; indeed, there was a good deal of talk about it in the housekeeper's room among the other upper servants. About this time the valet of a great foreign duke, who happened to be also staying in the neighbourhood, and himself a foreigner, came to me one day when I was very downhearted, and asked me to come over to the great house where he was staying and drink a bottle of Rhine wine with him. I went, and he showed me your advertisement, and told me he thought it would be a good thing for me.

"I thought so too, but I did not believe that you would be likely to take me if you were told why I was leaving the Dook, as I have no doubt you would have been.

"I mentioned this to the foreign valet, and he said he thought he knew a gentleman who would help me, and perhaps I had better go and see him first. By his direction, sir, I went to see a gentleman at the Langham Hotel in London, a Mr. Saumarez."

"Saumarez?" I exclaimed. "What was he like?"

"He was a dark gentleman, sir, and he had got

something the matter with one of his eyes."

"Thank you," I said, "go on. I think I know who the gentleman was."

"He asked me to confide in him, sir, and I told him everything, and the difficulty I feared I should have in finding another situation.

"After some conversation he said he thought I certainly ought to try for your situation, and that if I succeeded to come and let him know, and he would see about the character without troubling the Dook.

"As you know, sir, you were good enough to entertain my application, and I then went straight away to Mr. Saumarez to ask him what I was to do.

"He said that on certain conditions a friend of his would give me a character."

"That was Captain FitzJames, I suppose?" I interrupted.

"Exactly, sir," Brooks replied, "the gentleman who you supposed I had been living with."

"This is pretty bad, Brooks," I said gravely, looking away at the grey horizon. In my heart I was thoroughly sorry for the man. And he was such a good valet, too! No wonder, for he had lived with one of the richest dukes in England.

"Yes, it is pretty bad, sir," he continued, "but not as bad as what's to come. I asked Mr. Saumarez what conditions he required of me, and he told me. First, I was to keep him informed daily of every movement of yours; secondly, I was to be ready to act under his orders in certain 'simple matters.' He explained that these simple matters would consist in 'little acts which would harm no one.'

"At first I was inclined to walk out of the room and leave him, and I think he saw my intention, for he held up his hand and went on further.

"He told me plainly that I was entirely in his power, and that he could prevent me getting a situation at all if he chose. I had told him I had a wife and two children depending on me – although I deceived you, sir, in that matter under his advice. He asked me now whether I wished them to starve. He pointed out that if I accepted his terms he would double my wages, so that I could leave my little family in comfort. I couldn't bear to think they would be in want, sir. I felt certain I had fallen among a bad lot, and believed myself to be powerless. In the end, sir, like a fool, I gave in and agreed to his terms.

"Now just listen, sir, how I betrayed you.

"I wrote every day to Mr. Saumarez and told him of every movement of yours, especially the going to the solicitors; he wanted to know all about that.

"You will remember the last time you went there, just before we went to Euston on our way to Liverpool? Well, that newspaper man running along and knocking me down, and the lady and gentleman coming up and brushing you down, was all a put-up job. I was told to fall down and keep out of the way to give the others time to act. Of course, it was they who cut your coat open.

"I wonder you can listen to me, sir."

"Go on," I said.

"I knew they hadn't got what they wanted, because there was a long telegram waiting for me at Liverpool on board, and I was told to keep up communication with Saumarez by Marconograms. So, I did; I did all they wished until the train was held up, and then, sir, when I saw you stripped by those greasers, and about being carried off, I could stand it no longer. I made my mind up to throw Saumarez over and protect you; it was then that I went and fetched your revolver and put it in your hand. Since then I have kept on giving them information, but it is all false.

"I couldn't bear the worry of it any longer. I laid awake all last night, and this morning I made up my mind to come and tell you everything.

"I know you will discharge me, sir, and I deserve it.

"I only have to humbly ask your pardon for betraying you, and forgetting I was once an English soldier."

He finished, standing before me, white, and with quivering lips. As he ceased speaking, I could not help remembering that, at any rate, he had saved my life in all probability, and that which was far dearer to me than life, the honour of Dolores.

I turned to him.

"For the present," I said, as kindly as I could under the circumstances, "continue to do your duties, and I will consider what I must do."

"If I could only think you would give me another chance, sir – – " he said, eagerly taking a step forward.

"I cannot promise," I said. "I must consider."

Chapter XVII. The Steel Safe

Don Juan's conduct upon our arrival in London was both a revelation and a surprise to me.

First, following a custom, now long established for diplomatists, he put up at Claridge's.

From that famous hotel I had the pleasure of accompanying him at his request on a series of visits.

The first was an appointment at the Foreign Office, and there he was closeted with the Secretary of State for a solid two hours, while I was kicking my heels in a waiting-room. His last words to me had been exceedingly disappointing.

"You must forgive me for not taking you with me, Anstruther," he said, "but the matter I am engaged upon is of such an exceedingly confidential nature that I dare not disclose it to any one, except the Ministers themselves."

I simply bowed my acquiescence and said nothing.

But being left alone in the waiting-room, which was liberally supplied with writing materials, I industriously filled up my time by writing letters.

First, of course, to Dolores, whom I had left but an hour before at Claridge's, and to whom I yet felt constrained to pour forth my soul on paper.

The feeling, I have no doubt, was a mutual one, as when I returned to my hotel to dress, there was handed to me as usual a letter from Dolores, giving me an account of her morning's proceedings.

Having disposed of my letter to her on this particular morning, I wrote to my cousin St. Nivel.

"As for solving the mystery of the old lady at Bath and her casket," I wrote, "whether she is alive or dead, and why she sent me to Valoro, *all*, my dear Jack, are to me at the present moment as great a mystery as the reason why His Serene Highness the Duke of Rittersheim should want to shoot me at a *battue* down in Norfolk!

"I go about with Don Juan d'Alta, and I might just as well be walking about with one of the lions in Trafalgar Square for all the information I get out of him. His is the silence of the old diplomatist."

To Ethel I sent my love; she was pretty well informed of our movements, as she and Dolores had become fast friends, and corresponded twice or thrice a week.

From the Foreign Office Don Juan walked me over to the Home Office, and there he had a lengthy interview with the Home Secretary of fully an hour's duration. Finally, we went to Scotland Yard, and there I thought we should never get away at all; I, of course, being "in waiting" all the time.

But there was one consolation which Dolores and I had had ever since we set foot on board the *Oceana* on our return, and that was, we did not care how soon Don Juan knew of our betrothal; we only waited for the old gentleman to be rid of his mysterious business to declare ourselves.

For myself, I had but little anxiety as to the result. I had caught him looking at us on board the steamer, when we were together, openly lovemaking, and his expression then had been wistful, but not unkind nor unfavourable. Therefore, I had great hope.

"If he will not give his consent, darling," my little sweetheart had whispered often in my ear, "I shall tell him that I will go and be a nun."

"But you *won't*, will you, little one?" I always asked anxiously, "you won't go and leave me?"

And then she would generally make the naïve confession –

"I would rather marry *you*, dear, than be a nun."

After ringing the changes between the Foreign Office, the Home Office, and Scotland Yard for a week, Don Juan suddenly expressed his determination to go down to Bath. I was asked to secure rooms for them at the "Magnifique"; it was to be a fairly long stay, and Dolores was going too.

The proceedings at Bath mystified me more than ever. The first thing that happened, when we were installed at the "Magnifique," was, that Inspector Bull accompanied the head of the police on a visit of ceremony and absolutely raised his hat to *me* on discovering that I was *à la suite* of Don Juan d'Alta! I was never more thunderstruck in my life, and was hardly able to return such an unexpected act of courtesy, through astonishment.

The next thing was a ceremonious visit to Cruft's Folly in a motor car. There we found the inspector keeping guard over a curious array of articles assembled on a table on the ground floor of the tower; they were a most extraordinary collection. First, there was a lady's handkerchief, and I identified it at once as a fellow one to that which I had found in the still warm bed of the old lady in Monmouth Street.

"Are you quite certain," inquired Don Juan, when I had told him about it in answer to his question. "Are you certain the handkerchief you found was like this?"

"As certain as I stand here," I answered; "if there is any doubt about it I can get the other, for it is only at the hotel."

"Very well," replied the old gentleman with an air of satisfaction, making a note in a book, "that settles that matter. Now for the next. Have you ever seen that silver cigarette box before?"

I took up the article he referred to, which was standing by the handkerchief on the table, and examined it; it might, or might not, have been that case from which I took a cigarette in the old lady's room on the occasion of my first visit. I told them so.

"You cannot swear to it?" asked the old Don.

"No," I answered, "I cannot swear to it; it may be the case, and it may not."

"Now, Inspector," he said, turning to the police officer, "kindly show Mr. Anstruther *that*."

He pointed to a bundle lying on the table, the last of the articles, and the inspector took it up, and slowly unfolded it. *It was a lady's quilted white silk dressing-gown, and the whole of the bosom of it was deeply stained with what was evidently dried blood.*

I turned in triumph to the police officer.

"*That* is the dressing-gown worn by the old lady the last time I saw her lying bleeding on her bed in the basement of 190 Monmouth Street. I told you of it at the time, and you would not believe it."

Don Juan appeared exceedingly interested at this exhibit, and leant over it with his gold pince-nez held to his eyes.

"Ah!" he remarked at last, removing his glasses with a sigh, "then I suppose that is all you have to show Mr. Anstruther, Inspector?"

The inspector gathered up the articles ceremoniously before he answered.

"That is all we 'ave to exhibit to Mr. Anstruther *at present,*" he said.

Mr. Bull was not going to commit himself.

From Cruft's Folly we went straight to 190 Monmouth Street, and there we found the sergeant's wife in her Sunday clothes to do honour to the occasion; the baby as usual dangled easily from her arm.

Descending to the basement, I was astonished to find a well-known gentleman waiting us in the room with so many sad remembrances for me.

This gentleman was a Mr. Fowler, and I knew him to be one of the Crown solicitors. His presence there, however, was accounted for when Don Juan asked me for the key of the steel safe, which I still had in my possession.

Under the circumstances I felt fully justified in giving it to him.

"Now, Anstruther," he said cheerfully, "I will get you to show me and Mr. Fowler the secret of the panel."

The broken glass had been already cleared from the frame over the mantelpiece; therefore, as soon as I touched the carved rose on the left-hand side, the framework moved up. I touched the spring beneath and the door in the wall flew open; there within was the steel safe, exactly as I had seen it last, Don Juan turned to me with a look of solicitude.

"Don't feel offended, Anstruther," he began, "at what I was going to say, but it is essential that I should open this safe in the presence of Mr. Fowler alone."

As he took the key from my hands and inserted it in the lock, I bowed and left them.

For half an hour I paced the passage without or wandered through the back door into the neglected garden, which I found abutted on a disused grave-yard – a very common object, met with often in star-tlingly unlikely places in one's walks in Bath.

It was on my return from one of these little rambles that I found the door of the old lady's sit-ting-room open, and Don Juan and Mr. Fowler su-perintending the removal of the safe by two porters; a third gentleman had now joined the party.

"This is Mr. Symonds of the Bank of England,"

said the old Don ceremoniously. "He has very kindly undertaken the removal of this safe to London."

I was getting now so used to the Don's mysterious movements that even this did not surprise me. I noticed, however, that the safe had been very carefully *sealed* in addition to being locked. The safe was carried up to the street and placed on the front seat of a large motor car which was waiting.

In this the representative of the Bank of England quickly entered, and two very unmistakable detectives who had been standing by mounted on the front seat, then the motor puffed away.

"They won't stop now," remarked Mr. Fowler, "until they reach Threadneedle Street."

Within a quarter of an hour Don Juan and I were back in his private room at the hotel.

"Thank God!" he exclaimed as we entered, "my mind is now cleared from that terrible anxiety, and I can rest in peace."

I looked very hard at the old gentleman as he sank into an arm-chair, but I did not agree with him.

"Excuse me, Don Juan," I said, "I have another very serious matter to trouble you with."

Chapter XVIII. The Old Graveyard

"What do you mean?" asked Don Juan.

The old man glanced at me quickly, an anxious look in his eyes.

I looked him straight in the face in return.

"Don Juan," I replied, "Dolores and I love one another."

The anxious look faded into one of softness, and he commenced walking backwards and forwards in the room, without answering me.

Presently he stopped and faced me again, and in his old eyes, which were blue like his daughter's, there were tears.

"I will not conceal from you, Anstruther," he began, "the fact that your affection for Dolores has been apparent to me for some time past, and has given me cause for much thought. Not that I have distrusted you, remember," he added with a kind glance.

"I am not often deceived in a man, and I think I could trust my child to you." I gave a great gasp of pleasure, but he added immediately, "under certain circumstances."

"And those circumstances?" I asked anxiously.

"First," he began as he sank into an arm-chair, "you are of different religions; you are not a Catholic, I understand."

I answered him smiling.

"I don't think we shall disagree over that," I replied, "Dolores and her children shall worship the Almighty as she wishes. My religion is that of a man of the world, I worship with all."

The old man nodded his grey head and smiled.

"I did not expect you to be very bigoted," he answered quietly.

"Now, there is another point, Don Juan," I continued, "upon which I must satisfy you, and that is my ability to keep a wife."

I told him of my little estate in Hampshire with its small manor house on the shores of the Solent, and how I had let it to a yachting man who had taken a fancy to it; it being too large for my modest bachelor wants. I told him proudly of my balance at the bank, swelled by the thousand of the old lady of Monmouth Street, of which he already knew. I told him what my income was from every source, and finally what I succeeded in wringing annually from the publishing body. This last item seemed to amuse him mightily, despite his polite effort to listen to me with becoming solemnity.

"Very good, very good, Anstruther," he said at last encouragingly, "I see you are quite capable of maintaining a wife in a modest way. It is very creditable to you, too, that you have taken to making money by your pen. With regard to Dolores, however, should she become your wife, she is not likely to be a burden to you financially. She will, in the first place, become entitled on her marriage to an income of fifty thousand dollars, which arises from property which I settled upon her mother.

"Then, she is my only child as you know, and I shall make a further settlement upon her. My income has been accumulating for years, I want but little; when I die she and her children will have *all*."

The amount he mentioned certainly took my breath away, but I raised my hand and asked him to stop.

"Believe me, Don Juan," I said, "I should be a happier man if I could supply her wants by the work of my hands."

"I *do* believe you," he answered, "and those would be my own sentiments exactly under similar circumstances. You will, however, not find a good income a bar to marital happiness if used judiciously. But enough of financial matters; I wish to come to another more important point. I believe it that Dolores loves you; from my own observations I believe she does, but I must hear it from her own lips.

"Should it prove to be the case, which I do not doubt, then I will give my consent to your marriage."

I rushed forward joyfully to thank him, for I knew what Dolores' answer would be, but he held up his finger to check me.

"I will give my consent under those circumstances," he continued, "on *one* condition."

"And that?" I asked eagerly.

He did not answer me at once; he sat in his chair, with his hand to his forehead, thinking.

Then he lifted his head.

"Sit down and listen to me, Anstruther," he said; "I want you to follow exactly what I say.

"When you arrived in Valoro six weeks ago, and gave me that casket, you reopened an episode in my life closed many many years ago."

He spoke with great emotion and his lip trembled. I even saw a tear coursing down his sunburnt cheek.

"Since then," he continued, "you have very kindly followed me in the fulfillment of certain duties which devolved upon me upon opening that packet. You have followed me without question, as became a gentleman, taking an old man's word that all was well. In keeping that silence of delicacy, Anstruther, you have unwittingly done me a great service; you have left me unhampered to fulfill that which I had to do."

He paused and placed his fingers together in deep thought.

"I place myself mentally," he continued, "in your position, and I try to think as you think – try to realise your feelings: the appeal you received from the old lady as she stood at the door of the house in Monmouth Street, your acceding to her request, your second visit, the discovery of the tragedy, the undeserved misfortunes that fell upon you in consequence, your fidelity to your promise to the lady who was at best a mere chance acquaintance, the impenetrable mystery which surrounds it all.

"I have thought of it, and I feel that you must be consumed with a great and reasonable curiosity.

"That you have not indulged that reasonable curiosity, that you have maintained a discreet silence under very trying circumstances has caused a very good first impression of you to grow into one of respect and strong regard."

He rose and took my hand in both his, the tears running down his cheeks.

"Anstruther," he continued, mastering his emotion with an effort, "I am going to ask a further sacrifice from you as a condition of my consent to your marriage with Dolores – a very necessary condition, or I would not make it.

"Anstruther, I ask you to keep eternal silence on what has occurred to you since you entered the door of the house in Monmouth Street, that dull evening in November. I ask you never to refer to it again from this moment, in any shape or form.

"Tell me, can you make this promise?"

I stood with my hand in his, my eyes fixed on his kind old face working with emotion.

"And this is the final condition you ask," I replied, "to my union with Dolores? You are satisfied in every other way?"

"I am satisfied," he replied; "I ask no more."

"Then I give you my promise," I replied, gripping his hand hard; "the subject to me shall be dead. God help me to keep my word!"

* * * * *

My future father-in-law and I sat chatting an hour longer over the bright fire in the sitting-room while the gloaming of a February day was deepening without, and he had talked to me with the familiarity accorded to one already admitted to his family circle.

Dolores had gone to a concert at the Assembly Rooms and we did not expect her back until between five and six.

It was when we had both paused in our conversation and sat with our eyes fixed on the leaping flames – the only illumination of the room – that a knock came at the door and a waiter entered.

"A gentleman to see you, sir," he said, addressing Don Juan.

"Who is it?" d'Alta asked.

"I think it is one of the police officers, sir," replied the man; "he gave the name of Bull."

"Ah! it's the inspector, evidently," commented the Don. "Show him up. I wonder whatever Inspector Bull can want," he continued, turning to me; "we only left him an hour or two ago."

The inspector came to answer for himself. The waiter threw open the door and he entered.

I saw at once that he had something of importance to communicate. His demeanour was that of the Duke of Wellington on the morning of Waterloo.

"Certain information of importance," he commenced, after we had greeted him, "having come to 'and this afternoon, sir, I thought it well to come round and see you immediate."

The inspector's eyes wandered round the apartment. There was a sideboard certainly; previous experience on former visits had, however, taught him to expect nothing from it. The foreign Don was evidently an advocate of temperance, like so many other foreigners who could not drink good, honest English beer – well seasoned with noxious chemicals.

"Indeed," commented Don Juan, who had received several of these mysterious visits before, and did not on that account expect much from this one. "What have you discovered?"

"It 'pears," continued the police officer, "that just after dinner to-day some children was playing in the little disused graveyard in the rear of 190 Monmouth Street."

From being a listless listener I became an earnest one immediately; an idea concerning that graveyard had crossed my mind that very morning while I contemplated its dismal gravestones, almost hidden in old rank grass, through the open ironwork forming the upper part of the gate which shut it off from the little strip of sloping garden in rear of 190 Monmouth Street. In my walk backwards and forwards, while I waited for Don Juan and the lawyer, Mr. Fowler, during their examination of the safe, I had come back to that iron grating again and again. It had somehow fascinated me.

"These 'ere children," proceeded the inspector, "was playing round the gravestones, and jumpin' over 'em to keep warm. It was while they were jumpin' and shovin' each other about over the graves that they noticed that the top stone of a great flat old grave was loose, and, of course, they started to make it looser by see-sawing it, until one fat boy jumped it a bit too 'eavy, and it tilted and let him in."

"In where?" I asked quickly.

"Into a new-made grave, sir," he answered solemnly – "a grave what had been dug recently under the old stone."

"Whatever for?" asked Don Juan.

"That's just where it is," replied the officer; "that's just what we want to find out. The grave is about half filled in with loose earth. We want to know what's under that loose earth, and that's why I'm here."

"What have we got to do with it?" asked the Don.

"The theory is, sir," replied Bull, "that *something* is buried under that loose earth. It may be stolen property. It may be a *body*."

I think both Don Juan and I whitened at the prospect disclosed by the inspector, but the Don soon recovered himself. He did not seem so affected by it as I imagined he would be.

"What do you propose to do?" he asked.

"We propose," answered the inspector, "to at

once have the loose earth cleared out and see what's underneath."

"Do you mean now?" I asked. "Why, it is quite dark."

"We mean to put two workmen on to dig out that earth at once, sir, and I want you and this gentleman, sir," he added, with a bow to the Don, "to come and be present. *There might be something to identify.*"

"Identify!" I exclaimed, rather horrified at the prospect; "what could we identify in the dark?"

"There'll be plenty of light, sir," answered Bull. "We shall bring half a dozen lanterns; besides, the moon will be up in half an hour's time."

I looked at Don Juan.

"Do you intend to go?" I asked.

The old man sprang to his feet.

"Though I believe the search may be a fruitless one," he answered, "I will miss no opportunity. I will certainly accompany the inspector."

The latter at once rose to his feet with a look of satisfaction on his large face.

"I thought you would, sir," he answered, with a broad smile; "but I should advise you, sir, if I might be so bold, to *wrop* up well, as the job may be a long-ish one, and them graveyards is very damp."

Don Juan rang the bell for his valet to fetch him a fur-lined overcoat, and I told the waiter to tell my man Brooks to bring mine.

At my suggestion, the Don ordered some liquid refreshment for the inspector. Scotch, cold, proved to be his selection, and he stood imbibing it, while we waited, commenting upon its excellent qualities for "keeping out the cold," a theory which I have since learned is totally erroneous.

Presently the coats came, and we followed the inspector down to the door of the hotel, where a closed fly was already awaiting us. We drove away through the brilliantly lighted city to the neighbourhood of long, dismal Monmouth Street on the hillside, but this time we did not drive down the street itself but took a turning which ran below it.

"The gate of the old burial ground," explained the police officer, "is in this street. It will be far more convenient to enter it this way than by going round by Monmouth Street."

At the old-fashioned, sunken iron gateway of the dreary looking, neglected graveyard a policeman was standing, apparently keeping guard.

He might have saved himself the trouble, for, with the exception of two poor-looking little children – one standing with his mouth open and a forgotten hoop and stick in his hand – the place was deserted.

We received the constable's salute and, passing through the rusty iron gate which he held open for us, came at once among the long wet grass and sunken, often lopsided, tombs. On the farther side of the ground another constable stood with a lighted lantern, and near him two labouring men, with spades and picks leaning against an old stone by them. These latter hastily put out their pipes as we approached.

I was curious to see what sort of tomb this was which had been apparently so desecrated, and followed the inspector towards it at his invitation.

"This is the grave I told you about, gentlemen," he said, indicating it with his finger; "you will see they have lifted the top stone off."

It was a very large tomb of the description called "altar tombs," but the flat stone which covered it lay by its side, and the rotten state of the low brickwork which had supported it accounted for its giving way, even with the boy's weight.

The inspector took a lantern and held it inside the broken brickwork; yes, there could be no doubt the grave had been disturbed, and that recently.

Freshly turned earth lay between the walls of brickwork, which were spacious enough to allow of an ordinary-sized grave being dug within them.

"Is the grave just as it was found?" I asked.

"Exactly, Mr. Anstruther," he answered. "The earth has not been disturbed at all. But I think we'll make a start now. Here comes Dr. Burbridge, the officer of health. We thought it better to have him present."

The figure of a man wearing a tall hat now appeared crossing the graveyard, preceded by a constable bearing a lantern.

After briefly introducing the newcomer, the inspector gave the word to the two labourers, and they scrambled inside the broken brickwork and commenced digging.

I looked round the weird spot as the noise of their spades became monotonous, relieved only by the throwing aside of the great lumps of moist earth; a mist was rising from the river flowing near, of which in the first stillness of our coming I could just catch the ripple of the water. It seemed to me that those who were long buried there had in life perhaps had some association with the river – even an affection for it – and had wished to be laid there near its soft murmur while they slept.

The men dug on and the pile of earth they threw up grew and grew; it was very clear that the old ground had been recently broken, and a new grave carefully shaped out of it. The sides were compact and firm and had not been disturbed, perhaps, for a whole century.

I glanced at the stone which had been removed, thinking, perhaps, that it might give me a clue to the date of the grave, but, alas, time and the weather had rotted the soft stone and it had come off in layers. The face of the stone was a blank, and the names of those who lay beneath lost for ever.

The moon had risen and the men had dug down perhaps four feet, but nothing had come to light. Then, as they were proceeding after a brief halt, one of them gave a cry.

"There's something here, marster!" he cried excitedly.

At the sound of his voice all the lanterns were brought to the edge of the grave, and we looked down into the hole, which the bright moonbeams did not reach. It was illuminated solely by the dull yellow light of one candle-lantern by which the men worked. The two diggers had withdrawn themselves, half scared, to the sides of the hole, and were looking down fearsomely at *something* at their feet. It appeared that they were afraid of treading upon this something; at first I could not tell what they were looking at, but presently my eyes became accustomed to the gloom. It was a dark patch protruding from the ground.

"What is it?" I asked the men, as we all hung over the edge of the brickwork.

The nearest man turned a white face up to mine and answered me.

"It's a human 'ead, sir," he said.

I think we all drew back again as he said this, and the doctor stepped forward with a flask in his hand.

"If you will take my advice, gentlemen," he said, addressing Don Juan and me, "you will have a nip of this old brandy before we go any further in this matter. Then I think you had better let me give the instructions to these workmen, Mr. Inspector, or they may do some damage unintentionally."

Don Juan touched me on the arm. His hand trembled fearfully.

"Let us come away and walk a little," he said; "the strain of this affair is too much for me."

I took his arm and walked away with him towards the gate, where now quite a little crowd had assembled, attracted by the lanterns round the grave.

Knowing the Don's fondness for smoking and its soothing effect upon him, I handed him my cigar case, and he took a cigar and lit it. There seemed to be something in the aroma of the fine Havannahs as I lit one, too, that dispelled the lurking mouldiness of the old burial ground.

"But for those children playing around that tomb this afternoon," remarked d'Alta, "this body might have lain there undiscovered for years. It was a cunning mind which thought of using an old grave as a receptacle for a fresh body."

We strolled backwards and forwards on the grass-grown pathway, and I kept the old gentleman as far as I could from the open grave. The voice of the doctor giving directions and the muffled answers of the men working in the excavation came to us occasionally.

Presently, as we turned in one of our walks, I saw the labourers had come out of the grave and were hauling at something, assisted by the two policemen.

As I checked the Don in our walk, and looked on, a white mass was raised from the opening and laid by the doctor's direction on an adjacent flat tomb.

I shuddered as I saw the whiteness of it in the moonlight, and my thoughts reverted to the blood-stained figure of the old lady which I had last seen lying on her bed in the house in Monmouth Street.

The workmen went down into the grave again, and Inspector Bull came towards us.

"Will you kindly step over this way for a few moments, Mr. Anstruther?" he asked. "I want to see if you can recognise the body which has been brought to the surface."

I let go the arm of Don Juan which I had been holding, and with a sickening feeling at my heart followed Inspector Bull. He led me towards the object lying on the old moss-grown tomb, and I could not summon the words to ask him who it was. There was a strong presentiment in my mind that I should look upon the dead face of the old lady at whose wish I had crossed the Atlantic.

We came to the body, over which a piece of sacking had been thrown, and this the inspector drew back, while one of the policemen held a lantern.

In its yellow light mingled with the clear moonbeams, I looked upon the face, and my heart gave a great leap of thankfulness. The face was perfectly fresh and recognisable. It was not the face of the old lady which I had feared to see, but that of a man with a coal-black beard, which seemed very familiar to me.

I had scarcely looked upon it when a cry came from the grave where the men were working, and they threw up a white bundle, evidently a bundle of linen.

This the inspector quickly opened, and displayed a heap of bedclothing and a pillow all stained with blood.

"Is that all?" asked the inspector, as the men jumped out of the hole.

"Yes, marster," the man replied, knocking the clay off his boots, "there's naught there now but the coffin of the old 'un, well-nigh moulderin' away, and the plate says he was one o' the old Mayors o' Bath."

I turned again to the exhumed body, and the recognition of it came to me in a flash.

It was the dark German who had helped to strap me in the chair in Cruft's Folly, when Saumarez was going to torture me.

Chapter XIX. The Struggle in the Tunnel

I was delayed two days in Bath by the inquest on the body of the German, the discovery of which in the old graveyard formed a nine days' wonder in the old western city and then died out altogether.

It was a very barren inquiry, for it discovered nothing. The man was a stranger, no evidence was produced to show who he was, and as an unknown stranger he was buried again, not in the old grave-yard, but in the new cemetery away among the hills.

There was only one piece of evidence which carried any interest with it, and that was the testi-mony of the doctor.

He stated that the man had been shot through the head and immediately killed; he produced the .450 revolver bullet which he had found in the head.

Furthermore, he added that the body had been buried at once, and by that means preserved from decay. It was practically incorrupt. It might have been buried there a month.

That was all, and all the coroner's acumen, and all the researches of the police, could produce no more. Public opinion had to be satisfied with a very vague verdict.

There was only one point of interest left for me in the matter, and that was the bundle of bed-linen which was found buried in the grave.

That was proved beyond doubt to be the bed-linen of my old lady of Monmouth Street; it was plainly marked with the letter C, surmounted on the case of the pillow by a small coronet.

"Things is coming round in a most extraordinary way to corroborate your statement about the old lady, Mr. Anstruther," remarked Inspector Bull patronisingly. "I could 'ardly believe it. I don't know when I come across another case like it."

I don't suppose he did. It was an enigma which puzzled many wiser heads than his in the long run; but I think the part which astonished him most was to be discovering, bit by bit, that the story of my visit to the house in Monmouth Street, as related to him and his brother, the "tip-top London detective," was actually founded at any rate on *some* fact!

The Don and I joyfully directed our respective servants to pack up for London at the conclusion of the inquest. Dolores had been sent back to Claridge's by her father, and placed under the care of Mrs. Darbyshire the morning after the discovery in the old graveyard. He had very wisely decided to keep her away from the gruesomeness of the inquest, which pervaded the whole town.

Under the circumstances that little interview which I was so anxious that he should have with her to discover the state of her affections towards me, was postponed, and things remained just as they were.

Nevertheless, I think both Dolores and I were perfectly satisfied to wait for the formal declaration of her father's sanction, being happy in the consciousness of each other's love and steadfastness.

So the inquest being disposed of, we very gladly went off to the station beneath the great cliff to catch the afternoon express to town.

We were in ample time, and strolled up and down the platform, taking a last look at the town which had proved so fateful to us both.

Presently the great engine, the embodiment of modern steam power, swept into the station, and the Don's man at once secured a first-class smoking compartment for us, with the aid of the guard, while Brooks looked after the luggage, the other man being a foreigner.

"I'm afraid I shall not be able to keep the whole compartment for you, gentlemen," said the guard civilly, as we took our seats; "but I'll put as few in as I can."

The old Don was the embodiment of politeness; he was the last person in the world to inconvenience any one on the railway or anywhere else, though he liked to have a carriage to himself when he could.

He told the guard so.

"I'll do my best, sir," replied the guard, with great *impressement*, as he pocketed Don Juan's five shillings. "You shall be inconvenienced as little as possible."

He locked the door and walked away, and I thought we should be left to ourselves.

The guard, however, had overestimated his powers.

The train was within a minute of starting when two passengers, evidently in a great hurry, made their appearance at the window. One was an old gentleman with a white beard, wearing blue spectacles, and apparently half blind; the other a young sturdy man, evidently his son, for the elder leant on his arm, and was addressed by him as "father."

The son led the old man straight to our carriage, and called aloud for the guard on finding it locked.

"Now, guard!" he cried with authority, when the official made his appearance, "open the door; all the other carriages are full."

"If you wouldn't mind coming down a few carriages farther, sir," suggested our guard, "I can find you two good corner seats at once."

"Open this door at once," cried the gentleman furiously; "there is only half a minute to spare, and don't you see my father is an invalid?"

Don Juan emerged from his corner with a look of genuine concern upon his face.

"Let the gentlemen in at once, guard," he ordered. "I would not be the cause of inconvenience to them on any account. Come in, gentlemen, I beg."

The guard opened the door, and the two passengers entered just as the stationmaster called out a remonstrance not to delay the train. The old gentleman sank back in his seat with a sigh of relief.

"I'm so glad we caught the train," he said breathlessly.

Brooks ran up at the last moment and handed our tickets to the collector, who had been waiting for them, as the train did not stop again until it reached Paddington.

As Brooks turned and touched his hat to us, it appeared to me that he started as he looked into the carriage, but the train was just off and the ticket collector almost pushed him into the next compartment to ours – a second, of course.

We puffed out of Bath, and I saw the last of its hills and stone houses for many a day; indeed, I don't think I have seen it since, except perhaps in the same way from a flying train. We were soon swallowed up by a great tunnel, and the Don and I subsided into thoughtfulness and the quiet enjoyment of our cigars.

Our fellow-travellers in the opposite corners maintained an absolute silence; they might have been two statues.

But in a few minutes we burst out again into the almost blinding daylight, and then it seemed to me that the appearance of the two men we were shut up with had undergone a change. It was, if not my fancy, a total change in the expression of their faces.

The idea seemed to fascinate me, and I kept my eyes fixed upon them both.

Presently, after a quick glance at his companion, the old man put his hand into the pocket of the thick travelling coat he wore and quickly pulled out a revolver; then in a voice which I knew again full well he addressed us both, at the same time covering Don

Juan with his pistol.

"If you make the slightest movement, or speak without my permission, I shall fire."

I saw as I sat looking at them that the younger man had also produced a revolver, and was covering me.

Then the two moved nearer us into the two central seats of the compartment, for the convenience, as it proved, of talking to us.

Don Juan and I sat petrified with astonishment, whilst the elder man spoke again. I knew him from the first moment he had opened his lips, despite his disguise, to be the Duke of Rittersheim, or "Saumarez," as he had called himself.

"Don Juan d'Alta," he began, "I know you very well, and I don't suppose you have forgotten me."

"I know your voice, *Your Serene Highness*," responded the old Don, with a distinct accentuation of the title.

"Very well," replied the Duke. "Then that knowledge will enlighten you to the extent that you will be aware that I want something of you."

Don Juan made no reply.

"I want," proceeded the Duke, "the key of the steel safe which you removed from 190 Monmouth Street, Bath, and sent to the Bank of England. I want also an order from you to the directors of the Bank of England, authorising them to give me access to the safe. My friend here has writing materials."

My glance turned to Don Juan, who was contemplating the Duke with a stony stare of contempt.

"You will get neither the key nor the order, sir," he replied.

The Duke shrugged up his shoulders.

"You will compel me, then, to take a certain course," he answered. "I believe you have the key with you?"

He was right, the Don had it, but neither of us answered him.

"You will not answer," he proceeded. "Very well; silence gives consent. I believe you have it.

"That being so, I give you five minutes by this watch to make up your mind, Señor. At the conclusion of that period, we shall shoot you both as I shot the German they have been making such a fuss about in Bath, and take the key if you don't give it up. I have no doubt whatever I can get some clever fellow to copy your writing and manufacture me an order.

"At any rate, neither of you will be in a position to prevent me."

I confess that my blood ran cold at his words, as he took his watch out with his left hand and laid it on the seat. All my visions of happiness with Dolores seemed melting into shadows of grim death.

Don Juan, however, kept perfectly calm; there was scarcely a twitch on his face as he answered, although the colour had fled from it.

"That is all very well, sir," he replied coolly; "but what are you going to do with our bodies? You will be discovered, tried, and executed."

The Duke laughed aloud.

"They don't execute Serene Highnesses," he replied; "but, at any rate, as you are curious about my safety, I will tell you. In a few minutes the train will run into a tunnel. There we shall shoot you.

"In half an hour's time, during which we shall have the discomfort of regarding your two dead bodies, the train will once more enter a tunnel, the last before we reach London, and invariably the driver slows down in it to negotiate a very sharp curve. There we shall cast your bodies out on to the line as soon as we are in the tunnel, and availing ourselves of the slowing down which will occur a few minutes later, we shall leave the train."

As he spoke, the train entered the tunnel he mentioned, and almost at the same moment I saw a face appear at the window on the farther side behind the Duke and his accomplice.

It was the face of Brooks – my servant!

At first he expressed great astonishment at the situation as he looked through the window, then he very clearly frowned to me to keep silence.

Covered by the rattling of the train in the tunnel he began very carefully to open the door.

"The minutes are passing, gentlemen," remarked the Duke, in a mocking tone. "I must beg of you to make up your minds."

He clicked his revolver lock as a gentle reminder; but as he glanced at us in triumph, Brooks crept into the carriage behind him, and in a flash, with a great spring, his two strong hands held down those of our assailants which held their pistols. It was a splendid act of judgment.

In a moment I sprang forward too, to aid him, and then began a fearful struggle, in which Don Juan could take but little part. The great endeavour of Brooks and myself was to prevent the men using their revolvers; with all our strength we held down their hands and rendered them powerless.

When it appeared to me we were getting the mastery of them, I heard the Duke gasp out some guttural remarks in German to his companion.

Then suddenly the latter released his hold of the pistol, leaving it in our hands, but his freed hand went to his breast and reappeared with a long knife in it.

I did not actually see the blow, but I heard Brooks cry out, and I knew that the man had struck him.

But meanwhile Don Juan had picked up the revolver and pointed it towards the two villains.

"Fly, Duke," he cried, "for the honour of your house, or I will kill you."

With a curse the Duke let go his revolver and cried out in German to his companion. Then in a moment the two slipped out of the open door of the carriage on to the footboard and disappeared. We saw them no more.

Don Juan and I turned at once to Brooks, who had sunk back with a groan on the cushions.

"Are you hurt, my poor man," asked the Don; "have they stabbed you?"

"Yes, sir," he answered faintly, with his hand to his side. "They've about done for me, but I'm glad I die fighting like a British soldier should. I'm glad I've wiped the old score out by saving my master and you, sir."

When a quarter of an hour later the train ran into Paddington poor Brooks lay back in a corner with set white face. He had had his wish; he had died like a British soldier.

Chapter XX. The Departure of the Duke

As Dolores and I had both anticipated, the result of her interview with her father on the subject of her affections was entirely satisfactory to us both. The Don expressed himself satisfied, too, with the consultation, and gave us his blessing in the good old-fashioned way still in vogue in Aquazilia, or at any rate among the adherents of the old monarchy. We knelt at his feet to receive it. The result was a paragraph in the *Morning Post*, as follows: –

"A marriage has been arranged, and will shortly take place, between William Frederick, only son of the late Sir Henry and Lady Mary Anstruther, and Dolores, only daughter of Don Juan d'Alta, for some years Prime Minister of the late Queen Inez of Aquazilia."

This announcement brought us a shower of congratulations and inquiries as to the date of the wedding.

That query I naturally left to Dolores to answer, and at my earnest solicitation she very considerately decided, having in view my intense impatience in the matter, that the paternal assent – with blessing – -having been given in the month of February, we should be married in April.

Yes, absolutely *married*! The idea took me greatly by surprise at first. I used to wake in the morning, and the thought would in a manner sweetly confront me. It was as if a little mischievous Cupid sat on the end rail of my bed and revelled in his work.

"William Frederick," he seemed to say, "you're going to be married. You're going to marry Dolores. What do you think of it?"

I *did* think a great deal of it, and the thought to me was ecstasy.

I often used to wonder, as I contemplated in my mind's eye this little wicked Cupid sitting on my bed, whether he went and sat in like manner on Dolores', and if he did, what the little imp of mischief said to her.

But time flew, long as the interval seemed at first between February and April.

I did not see half as much of my Dolores as I could have wished; Mrs. Darbyshire and a host of other ladies absorbed her.

After a week or two my cousin Ethel joined her sage counsels to the rest in the matter of the bridesmaids' dresses. She herself was to be the chief of that important band, to which sundry male recruits in the shape of small boys were to be added by way of pages.

I never could quite gather how Ethel took my engagement. Her congratulation assumed the form of a short note.

"Dear Bill," it ran, "so you've done it!

"Well, dear old fellow, I saw it was a dead certainty at Valoro, and I congratulate you both and wish you every happiness with all my heart.

"Dear little Dolores is a right good sort, and if I

were a man I think I should fall in love with her my-self. I am sure she will make you happy; mind you take care of her!

"There is one thing I am sure you will be glad to hear.

"Give her a season or two over an easy country to begin with, and I assure you she will ride to hounds as well as any girl born and bred in the Shires. Believe me, dear Bill, I am speaking seriously, and you know me too well to think I would deceive you on such a matter.

"I leave you to teach her to shoot; I think every girl should be able to handle a gun; it gives her something to talk about to other girls' brothers."

This was the gist of the letter, and I put it aside with a sigh, wondering whether dear old Ethel would ever marry herself. In that mood, I regretted that I had ever lingered in those dear old corridors at Bannington when the moonbeams slanted through the mullions of the narrow old Tudor windows, and Ethel came down the broad oaken staircase with a look of well simulated surprise in her eyes at finding me there, dressed early for dinner and waiting for her to surrender those red lips of hers in a cousinly kiss.

Cousinly?

Well, regrets were unavailing; I could not call the kisses back again, and how was I to know I was going to meet Dolores and of course fall straightway in love with her?

That is the way a man argues himself into a comfortable state of mind when his half forgotten peccadilloes of meanness spring up and prick him!

St. Nivel came round daily with his sister, and, to use his own expression, "took me in hand." This taking in hand meant principally marching me off to the tailors and hosiers to order new clothes.

"A man when he is going to be married," he said sententiously, "must make a clean sweep of all his old clothes and start afresh. It's a duty he owes to his future wife – and his tailor!"

He of course elected himself my best man, and only regretted that I was not in the "Brigade" that a dash of colour might be added to the ceremony by lining the church with his dear "Coldstreamers."

He was, however, getting tired of the Army. He confided to me his intention to "chuck it" at an early date, and devote himself to a country life entirely.

"In fact," he added, summing up the whole situation, "I mean to buy pigs and live pretty," whatever that expression might mean. His ideas of matrimony were, however, almost entirely of a pessimistic order, as he was for ever slapping me on the back and urging me to buck up, mistaking those delicious love musings which, I suppose, every bridegroom indulges in for fits of depression.

"My dear children," said the old Don to us one day, when we were all together, he, Dolores, and I; "my dear children, I want you to make me a promise."

"Of course we will, Padré," we both answered. "What is it?"

The "Padré" and the "dear children" were now well established forms of address, and I think the old man delighted in them.

"I want you to promise me," he replied, "that you will spend *some* part of the year with me in Valoro."

"Of course we will," we chorused.

Dolores whispered a few words in my ear to which I readily nodded assent.

"Padré," she continued aloud, "we will come and spend Christmas and the New Year with you, and we will bring Lord St. Nivel and Ethel with us. I am sure they will come. Then," she added, turning to me, "we will have all our courtship over again."

In such happy thoughts the time sped away. Don Juan, as an act of gratitude for what he called "a dutiful acquiescence" to his wishes, purchased a town house for us in Grosvenor Square.

"During the season," he added meditatively, "perhaps you will find a little room for me" – most of the best bedrooms measured about 25 by 40 – "that is all I need. After consideration, I have decided that it would be too much to ask you to have any of my dear snakes. If I bring any with me, I shall board them out at the Zoo."

The tenant of my manor house by the Solent, when he heard I was going to be married, called upon me at my club.

"My dear fellow," he said, "I'm a sportsman; I couldn't think of keepin' on your house when I know you'll want it to settle down in. I've seen another across the water that'll suit me just as well, and you shall have your own again before the weddin'."

He was a kind-hearted man and sent me a wedding present – a silver bootjack to take off my hunting boots with. He said it might be useful to both of us, which was a distinct libel on Dolores' dear little feet.

At last the eve of our wedding came and Claridge's Hotel was filled from basement to roof, principally with the relatives of both families. For a bevy of Dons with their wives and daughters, all kindred of my little Dolores, had crossed the Atlantic, glad of the excuse to visit London, and a contingent from France of the old *noblesse*, her mother's relatives, had arrived to do honour to the nuptials of the little heiress. And because she was already a large possessor of the goods of this world they brought more to swell it; gold, silver, and precious stones in such quantities that it took two big rooms at Claridge's to contain them, and four detectives to watch them, two by day and two by night.

But among these presents were two which puzzled me greatly – they came anonymously – a *rivière* of splendid diamonds for Dolores, a splendid motor car for me.

Had she been but a poor relation I fear her display of wedding gifts would have been but a meagre one. As it was, perhaps St. Nivel's terse comment on the "show," as he called it, was nearest to the truth.

"Bill," he said confidentially, "all this splendour is simply *barbaric*."

But nobody grudged little Dolores her grand wedding, nor the magnificent gifts, for every one loved her.

I was sitting calmly at breakfast on the morning of the day preceding our wedding, with my mind filled to overflowing with the happiness before me, when St. Nivel burst in upon me.

"Look here, Bill," he cried, flourishing a newspaper before my eyes. "Look here, *some one* has got his deserts at last!"

I took the paper from him and read the paragraph he pointed to; it was headed –

"Tragic Death of the Duke of Rittersheim."

I paused, put down the newspaper, and looked at St. Nivel.

"Yes," he said, interpreting my look; "you will be troubled with him no more in this world; he's dead. Read it and see."

I took up the paper and read on –

"MUNICH, *Tuesday*.

"Considerable consternation was caused this morning in the Castle of Rittersheim and its neighbourhood upon the fact becoming known that His Serene Highness the Duke had passed away during the night. It appears that the Duke has been in bad health ever since his return from England two months ago, where he had the misfortune to break

213

his arm; he suffered also the loss of a very dear friend, in Mr. Summers, an American gentleman who, for some time, had been acting as his secretary, and whose body, it will be remembered, was found under very mysterious circumstances, at the time the Duke left England, in a tunnel on the Great Western Railway, just after the Bath express had passed through, in which train it is known Mr. Summers had been travelling with an elderly gentleman. A rumour concerning the connection of Mr. Summers with a murder which had taken place in the Bath train seems to have preyed on the Duke's mind, and he has been unable to sleep for some weeks past.

"It is presumed that for this reason he had commenced the habit of injecting morphia, as a large hypodermic syringe, with an empty morphia bottle, were found beside his dead body. The general opinion is, that he succumbed to an overdose."

"Well, what do *you* think," asked St. Nivel, as I laid down the paper, "accident or suicide?"

"It is impossible to say," I replied. "Nobody can tell, and I should think that will be one of the problems which will go down to posterity unsolved."

"As unsolved, I suppose," he answered, "as the mystery of your old lady of Bath?"

That was a subject I had barred since my pledge to Don Juan. "Who can tell?" I answered with a shrug of the shoulders, "I have given it up. I never think of it."

"*I* do, though," replied my cousin, "and I also recollect, very often with mingled feelings, the way in which the finding of that man Summers' body in the tunnel was hushed up, and no further efforts made to connect him with the murder of poor Brooks."

"I don't see that any good purpose would have been served," I answered, "if they *had* connected him with it. He could not have been tried and hanged."

"No, certainly not, but there would have been the satisfaction in *knowing*. But I believe your deceased friend the Duke of Rittersheim worked that. In my opinion he threw a cloak of some sort over the Bath case too, and I don't suppose you will ever discover the truth of it."

"No," I answered solemnly, "I don't suppose I ever shall."

And I don't suppose I ever should but for one of those little chances which occur in a man's life, trifles in themselves, but leading on to great discoveries.

The next day after that little talk, amid the pomp of a great wedding, almost regal in its magnificence, I took Dolores to be my little wife, to have and to hold from that day forth in sickness and in health, for richer, for poorer, until death we two doth part.

And from that time I walked as on air, and forgot the murky clouds which had darkened my horizon in the days before I found my happiness.

Chapter XXI. Madame La Comtesse

It was five years after my marriage, or to be correct, in May of the year nineteen hundred and seven, that Dolores and I, leaving our three dear little children in the manor house on the shores of the Solent whilst we took a flying trip to Switzerland, found ourselves one heavenly spring morning standing on the balcony of the great hotel at Lucerne which is built on the very edge of the blue lake.

"Well, where shall we go to-day, darling?" I asked my little wife as I slipped one hand round her waist and took the cigar from between my lips with the other; "shall we ascend grim Pilatus, or cog-wheel it up the Rigi and have lunch at the little hotel at the top, or shall we idle away the day in a boat on the lake? What say you, little one?"

An old German passing below with his hand behind his back, feeling his way gingerly along on gouty feet with the aid of a stick, looked up, smiled, and shook his head at us. He took us for a newly married couple!

When the laughter provoked by this little interlude had subsided, I once more put the question to Dolores.

"Where shall we go to-day?"

"Darling," she answered, "I'm entirely for the lazy day on the lake. I want to be idle."

So the lazy day on the lake it was.

A small hamper containing a cold chicken,

some ham, a salad, with other accessaries for lunch, and the added luxury of a gipsy tea-set, having been duly put into a boat, we followed it, and taking our seats, were met with the following query of the boatman, who sat looking at us, his two oars poised ready for work –

"Where will you go?"

We exchanged a significant glance, then gave voice simultaneously to the thought which was in both our minds.

"Anywhere."

The boatman nodded sagaciously; here again he even – the experienced – was deceived into believing that he had charge of a pair who had recently sworn to keep each other warm for life.

Had he been asked for his opinion concerning us, his reply expressed in his native tongue would have been briefly –

"Honey mooners!"

As I had reason to believe, after finding that we were perfectly indifferent as to where we went, he decided to have a little trip to suit his own convenience. He would go and see his sister at the Convent of The Nativity up the lake.

He continued sagely nodding his head as he rowed us away, and in reply to a question of mine as to what direction he had decided on, winked confidentially.

"Monsieur et madame," he replied, "leave it to

me. You will have a great surprise."

We did, but not in the way he intended.

On the dark face of the boatman as he worked steadily up the lake I saw both perplexity and concern; first, although I held Dolores' hand, as I usually did on such occasions when we were alone – or nearly so, for the Swiss oarsman counted for little – yet the man saw no yearning desire on my part to *kiss* her, as was the case with most husbands in the early days of the *lune de miel*.

Several times I noticed that he gave me opportunity by turning round and straining his neck to see imaginary obstacles in the way for the fulfilment of this custom, which, to his surprise, I did not avail myself of. There were no blushes, no abrupt separations, and no assumed looks of unconcern when he turned round again.

The situation was a puzzling one. But there was a pale cast of thought over his features in addition, which I only knew the reason for later on. He was puzzling his brains to find an excuse for taking us to the very plain looking convent up the lake which, although beautifully situated, yet presented no extraordinary attractions beyond a well ordered and ancient garden, laid out in terraces on the side of one of the lower slopes of the mountains, and, of course, the beautiful view. Therefore when, at that curve in the lake when the Rigi comes into fullest view, a smile of satisfaction overspread the boatman's face, I knew, after, that he had solved the difficulty and found the excuse for taking us to such a very ordinary resort.

"I will show these simple English people," he had reasoned, "the long-haired goats. I will make a *spécialité* of these animals for the delectation of this cold-blooded bride and bridegroom, who do not kiss when I turn round to observe the prospect."

In the course of an hour and a half we arrived off a white terrace-like landing place with a flight of steps leading down to the lake.

All questions as to our destination had been answered by the boatman with mysterious nods and winks, giving promise of a stupendous surprise in store. His object was to get us safely on shore before he opened the subject of the hairy goats, lest we should, insular like, change our minds and not give him the opportunity of visiting his sister. The boat shot alongside the steps, the man sprang out and assisted us to land; a nun who had been working in the garden came down and met us.

"*Ma soeur*," explained our boatman, "this English milor and his lady have a great desire to see your most splendid goats!"

The good sister looked surprised, an expression which Dolores and I shared with her, mingled with amusement. We had, however, no particular objection to inspecting her goats, notwithstanding.

"Our Mother," she replied amiably, "I am sure, will be pleased to show monsieur and madame the goats if it will give them any gratification."

She preceded us through the beautifully kept kitchen garden, and up a flight of steps to another above, each foot of the productive soil being used to advantage, as we saw by the abundance of the crops reared on the sunny slope.

We mounted up from garden to garden until we came to a large terrace full of flowers, which surrounded the conventual buildings and commanded a magnificent view of the lake.

Here the sister left us.

"Will monsieur and madame divert themselves here," she asked, "while I go fetch our Mother?"

Delighted with the beautiful surroundings and the glorious stretch of blue water below us, Dolores and I were quite content to enjoy the lovely scene by ourselves; our boatman had long since slunk off down a side alley to find his relative the lay sister.

We had walked half the length of the broad terrace absorbed in the view, when, turning from it, we became aware that we were not alone. At the farther end of the terrace was an old lady sitting in an invalid's chair, also enjoying the beautiful prospect. By her side sat a nun on a garden chair, holding a large white sunshade over her; the sun was very hot. Not wishing to disturb her privacy, we turned back and met the Reverend Mother approaching with our conductress.

She was amiability itself. Certainly she would show monsieur and madame the goats. She was unaware that they had become so celebrated. Perhaps monsieur and madame kept goats in England?

"No; you have come only by the recommendation of the boatman, Fritz Killner?" she asked. "No doubt he wished to give you the diversion of the long passage in the boat."

I saw a look of amused intelligence pass over the Reverend Mother's face; she had divined the object of the boatman's visit. In fact, she frankly told us later – when we had seen the goats – that he had a sister in the community, and thus let the cat out of the bag.

We were not by any means petrified with astonishment at the goats; they seemed very ordinary animals, but with very long white coats. I had seen better in a goat chaise at Ramsgate.

But we had, at the Reverend Mother's solicitation, to make the tour of the convent.

We inspected the cows, the pigs, the orchard and a very respectable range of glass houses.

Then we went to the chapel, and finally to the refectory; here the hospitality of the white-clad order burst forth; we must have *déjeuner*.

The good Superior waved aside the mention of our cold fowl, and insisted on cutlets and an omelette. Meanwhile, we were to walk with her upon the terrace to improve our appetite – we were simply ravenous already.

"I have brought you to the terrace, monsieur and madam," proceeded the nun, "not only to admire the fine view and increase your appetites, but also to present you to Madame la Comtesse."

"Madame la Comtesse?" I repeated inquiringly.

She indicated the old white-haired lady sitting at the farther end of the terrace.

"That is Madame la Comtesse, the founder of this religious house," she explained. "She delights to see English visitors. She adores your nation. Come, let us go to her, but I ask you to approach quite near her, or she will not see you clearly. She is short-sighted."

Walking one on either hand of the Reverend Mother, we approached Madame la Comtesse.

The attendant nun had fixed the large white sunshade in a socket in the invalid chair; she was writing at the old lady's dictation. We came quite near before the Comtesse heard us approaching. Then she turned her head and looked at us, her kind old features breaking into a very sweet smile; her glance wandered from the Mother Superior to Dolores, then to me; there it stopped.

A little more frail, a little paler, yet with a bright colour in her cheeks, her still clear eyes gazing up to mine with an alarmed look in them; I knew her.

From the very first moment that she moved in her chair and turned to us; from the instant that that movement of her head disarranged the silk scarf which was wrapped round her throat, and laying it bare, showed a broad red scar upon it, *I knew her*; knew her for my dear old lady of Monmouth Street, Bath, at whose bidding I had crossed the Atlantic and endured many perils. I knew her, and as I gazed upon her her lips moved and formed two words –

"Mr. Anstruther!"

Chapter XXII. The Queen's Error

The Reverend Mother looked from Madame la Comtesse to me, and from me back again to the Comtesse.

"Madame," she said, addressing her, "without doubt you are old friends; here is a re-union of the most pleasant!"

We heard her words, both of us, I have no doubt, but we did not answer her; my thoughts were back again in that basement room at Monmouth Street. I saw "Madame la Comtesse," this healthy, bright looking old lady, lying on the disordered bed, her clothes soaked in blood, a great wound in her throat.

How did she come here?

How did she escape?

Those were the two questions which, for the moment, absorbed my whole faculties.

Her face, as I gazed upon it, expressed first blank amazement and alarm; then pleasure; finally the formation in a strong mind of a great resolve; she was the first to recover her entire self-possession, which, perhaps, she had really never lost.

"Mr. Anstruther," she said in English, extending her frail, delicate looking hand, "I am delighted to meet you again."

She took my hand in both of hers, and still holding it looked up into my face.

"You are well," she said, "I can see that, and happy. So you should be with such a charming wife. Please present me to her."

Dolores wanted no presentation; I think she loved the dear old lady at the very first sight. She went to her and gave her both her hands, and the Comtesse drew her face down to hers and kissed her.

"Your good husband did me a great service once, my dear," she said, "perhaps the greatest service a man can do a woman."

Dolores looked down at her wonderingly, and then at me.

"I wish I could tell you what it was, my dear," she continued, "but it is a secret. Still, perhaps your husband will tell you, *when I have told him*. I do not think that he realised the great benefit he did me at the time, for the good reason that he did not know its extent."

Dolores nodded her head and smiled, but I am sure she did not understand. How should she? I did not understand myself.

Our hostess, the nun, stood looking from one to the other of us with a smile on her face of that fixity which denoted that she did not understand a single word of what we were talking about.

Madame la Comtesse noted her isolation at once.

"Pray forgive me, *chère mère*," she said, breaking into French, which she pronounced with a very charming accent. "Mr. Anstruther and I are old friends. I meet madame, his wife, for the first time today."

In voluble language the Reverend Mother expressed her gratification at so happy a re-union, and in the midst of her compliments a nun arrived to say that *déjeuner* was served.

"Go to your lunch, my dears," the Comtesse said, "you must be famished after your long row on the lake." We had told her of our morning excursion. "Come back to me here afterwards," she continued, "if you will, and perhaps I will tell you that which you had a right to know long ago. Go now, and come back to me. I shall be under those trees yonder in the little arbour, which is cool in the heat of the afternoon."

Dolores and I went off to our *déjeuner*, but though it was excellent, we ate but little; we were thinking of the Comtesse.

"What a dear old lady she is," commented my warm-hearted little wife. "I don't think I have ever seen any one with such a sweet expression as she has!"

Neither had I, save, of course, Dolores.

"But whatever can she have to say to you, Will?" she continued, "and what is this great service you have done her?"

Alas, I could not tell her! I remembered my promise of eternal silence, made to her father before our marriage.

A cold muteness fell upon us both when I shook my head and did not answer her; it was the first time that the barrier of secrecy had arisen between us. The air of the room seemed cold as we sat there, though the sun shone brilliantly without. The fruits the nuns had placed before us at the end of our meal remained untouched.

"Coffee will be served to you on the terrace, monsieur and madame," announced our attendant nun, "it is the wish of Madame la Comtesse."

We arose silently, and went forth on to the sunlit terrace again, with its wealth of flowers and perfumed air. We walked without a word passing between us, and we came to the arbour in the shade overlooking a grand stretch of blue lake; here was the Comtesse, a table before her with coffee and liqueurs, amongst them a sparkling cut-glass decanter of yellow Chartreuse. A nun stood ready to pour out the coffee, the same that had written at the old lady's dictation and held her sunshade in the morning. She served us with our coffee, then with a low bow disappeared.

"Sister Thérèse," remarked the Comtesse, "is a great comfort to me; she writes all my letters and waits on me as if I were her mother."

At the word "mother" the old lady paused, and I saw her blue eyes fixed on a distant sail on the lake, with a sad, almost yearning look in them.

But in a moment it was gone. She turned to us, smiling.

"You must take a glass of Chartreuse," she said,

filling the tiny glasses, "it is so good for you. It is a perfect elixir!"

We drank the liqueur more to please her than anything else; then Dolores rose. I have never seen such a look of pain on her sweet face as was there then. God send I never see such again!

"No doubt, Madame la Comtesse," she began, "you wish to speak to my husband alone?"

The old lady glanced up at her for a few moments without speaking, there was a slightly puzzled look in her kind blue eyes; then, in a second, this look was gone, and one of deep solicitude and affection took its place.

It was as if some expression or passing glance on my dear wife's face had touched a chord somewhere in her nature, perhaps long forgotten.

She put out her slender white hand and drew Dolores down beside her on to the bench on which she sat; then she put her arm round her and pressed her to her, as one fondles a child.

"My dear," she said, "between a husband and his wife there should be no secret. No secret of mine shall divide you two. What I tell to one, I tell to both. What does it matter? For myself, I shall soon be gone; for the others, what harm can it bring them?"

We sat in silence, she with her arm round Dolores, her eyes fixed on the blue lake, a tear trembling in each, and she spoke to us as one whose thoughts were far away among the people and the scenes she described. I sat enthralled by every word she uttered.

"My eyes first saw the light," she began, "in a castle among the mountains around Valoro, one of the seats of my father, the king!"

Though I started at her words, they did not amaze me; I was prepared for them.

"My mother died when I was ten," she continued. "How I remember her with her fair curls and blue eyes, they seemed so strange among the dark-skinned Aquazilians! Young though I was, the shock of her death was the most awful, I think, that I ever had, perhaps – save one. It was all the greater because I had no brother or sister to share my grief with me. Yet I loved my father very dearly; he was a good and great man, and much reverenced by his people. There was no talk of revolutions nor republics in those days; the people were content under a mild rule.

"The years went on, and I became a woman, nurtured in the magnificence of a rich palace, yet imbued with the fear of God, for my father was a good man, and had me well taught my faith. I grew up, I think, with the brightness of my dead mother's spirit pervading me, for I avoided many of the pitfalls of youth.

"My royal father, often taking my face between his hands, would look into my eyes, and thank God that I had not in me the wickedness of the Dolphbergs, the race from which we sprang. It was when I was three-and-twenty that a sudden chill, caught by my father when out hunting, produced a fever which robbed me of him, and I was left an orphan; an orphan queen to reign over a nation.

"I was my father's only child; there was no Salic law to bar me. But as the orphan is ever succoured by heaven, so was I in my lonely royal state upheld by the counsels of a good and great man.

"Your grandfather, my child," she continued turning to Dolores, "the old Don Silvio d'Alta.

"He had been my father's stay in all his troubles; the d'Altas were a race of diplomatists, and when death claimed him your father, Don Juan, took his place."

A soft look came into her eyes as she sat with Dolores' hand in hers, a far-away look; her thoughts were in the times she spoke of.

"Those were happy days, Dolores," she continued, "those first years when your father and I ruled the people of Aquazilia. I had had a reign of ten years when your grandfather died and young Don Juan took the reins of government as my adviser; no one ever thought of contesting his right to it. Was he not a d'Alta?

"He was but twenty-five and I barely nine years older when he became my chancellor, and those ten years of ruling should have taught me prudence as a queen had I but listened to Don Juan's counsels too. For I know he loved me, loved me far too well perhaps and above my deserts.

"Had I had the prudence of an honest milkmaid who guards her honour as by instinct, I might have reigned this day at Valoro, instead of being the victim of a villain who, creeping into my heart like the serpent into Eden, destroyed it with the fire of burning love, and left me only ashes."

* * * * *

"It was in the very first year of Don Juan's chancellorship that there came to Valoro the son of a Grand Duke of one of the German States; what brought him there I shall never know. He told me it was the sight of my face in a picture, and the 'glamour of my virgin court,' but I think rather it was the spirit of the adventurer, or the gamester, which seeks for gain and counts not the cost to others. The Prince of Rittersheim – – "

"Rittersheim!" I exclaimed, interrupting her.

"Yes," she continued, "Adalbert, the eldest son of the Grand Duke of Rittersheim, he who succeeded his father two years later.

"The Prince was, I think, the handsomest man I have ever seen, and I think the wickedest. His tall fine presence, set off by a magnificent uniform, was seen at every Court I held. At every Court ball he claimed my hand for the first dance; as far as my lonely state allowed he sought me at every opportunity, and I, like a fool, was flattered by his attentions.

"Yes, to my sorrow, I began to love him.

"I had travelled but little; travelling was harder in those days; one tour in Europe with my father, that was all.

"I had fondly imagined that my suitor was a free, unmarried man. The first shock of his perfidy came when I learned he was not; but it came too late – I loved him.

"Don Juan told me, as he was bound in duty and honour to tell me from his position, that the Prince of Rittersheim was already married, but was separated from his wife.

"At the very next opportunity I had of speaking to the Prince – it was in a secluded part of the palace gardens, and the meetings were connived at by one of my ladies, the Baroness of Altenstein – I asked him plainly if he were married.

"This was apparently the opportunity he had been waiting for; he threw himself at my feet, and in passionate terms declared his love for me.

"He had loved me from the first moment that he had seen my portrait, he had loved me ten times more since he had seen the original.

"I stayed the torrent of his words and reminded him that he was married.

"Yes, he admitted he was married in name, but his marriage was no marriage; he had separated from his wife by the direction of the Grand Duke, his father – in this he spoke the truth, but the reason was far different – his so-called marriage was soon to be set aside as null and void, he told me.

"'Then come back to me when you are free,' I answered, 'and I will listen to you if the Church permits,' for I knew he was not of my Faith, and the

German States treated marriage lightly. My answer only caused him to redouble his entreaties; he begged me not to drive him from me, he could not live away from my presence, and I, poor fool, looking down at his handsome face and graceful person, and loving him with my whole heart, believed him.

"I know not how it came about, but I found myself sitting on a seat in that secluded corner of my garden with the Prince beside me with his arms around me, whilst my lady-in-waiting, the Baroness d'Altenstein, had discreetly wandered off out of earshot, but still with a keen eye that no one should disturb us.

"I never can account for it, I never can understand how it was I listened to him. I suppose it was the hot bad blood of the Dolphbergs which lurked in my veins and urged me, for I loved with all the passion of my race then; loved as a woman over thirty loves who has never loved before.

"Sitting on that rustic seat with him, whilst the cool evening wind played about us, I listened to a scheme he unfolded to me. He said he loved me to such distraction that he could not leave me, it would kill him; he could not wait until his marriage was set aside. He swore that he believed himself conscience free to marry, and swore a great oath that nothing should ever part him from me.

"In soft, loving whispers, he proposed that we should be married secretly; he had a priest all ready willing to perform the ceremony.

"Then he would be sure of me and could live

content.

"In a few months his former alliance would be set aside; before all the world we could be married again. A grand state ceremony if I would have it so.

"I listened to him, and my heart beat high as he spoke, yet I doubted in my saner moments whether I should ever be permitted to marry him by my ministers and my people were he free that very day.

"Poor fool that I was, he bent me to his will within a week, and he had no greater advocate for his cause than the Baroness d'Altenstein, my lady, though, poor soul, she only meant me well. But she was romantic, and had not long been married to a man she loved, a courtier from the country of the Dolphbergs; she had spent her honeymoon in their capital, and was an advocate for love at any price.

"Knowing I loved the Prince of Rittersheim, she worked only to make me happy by a marriage with him.

"With her knowledge only, I slipped away from Court for a week and went through a ceremony of marriage with the Prince at a little village church hidden away in the mountains a hundred miles from Valoro.

"I married him in the dress and under the name of a simple peasant woman, not knowing – as he did – that such a ceremony was utterly null and void.

"Was I happy? I think he loved me then – a little." A soft, sad look overspread the sweet old face; she gazed away across the lake in silence for a few moments. It seemed that, even after all these years, that time of love and falseness held some tender recollection still.

She came, as it were, to herself almost directly, and heaving a great sigh, went on –

"Long before the week was ended, the Prince had told me I must return to the Court, and take my place there as before.

"Of course I protested, and begged him to even then make our marriage public; that I would give up the throne. Had I not a great fortune left me by my father?

"Yes, that was the point that touched him, the great fortune. The treasures of my late father were immense. Besides an enormous fortune in money, mostly invested prudently in Europe, he possessed some of the most valuable diamonds in the world. It had been his diversion to collect them; he believed that they were always a most valuable security, likely to increase in value, and therefore he did not grudge the money sunk in them. The most valuable, reckoned to be worth a million English pounds, were stored in a safe of special construction made of steel. They were apart from the Crown Jewels, and were never worn. Indeed most of them were unset. My father's theory was that they were of immense value and could be carried in a small compass in case of necessity.

"The Prince, of course, knew from me full well of these treasures, and I firmly believe hungered for their possession from the very moment he learned from my foolish lips of their existence. He forced me at the end of the few days' honeymoon to return to the Court, and then from that time forth I saw him only surreptitiously with the aid of d'Altenstein, who was the aider and abettor of it all, yet loving me, and working only, as she thought, poor soul, for my happiness.

"I was soon undeceived in my Prince. I soon learned that he was in sore straits for money, and that he intended to get it from me.

"I gave him all I could, but he was insatiable. Finally he would come to me drunk and strike me when I could not meet his demands for thousands upon thousands.

"It was then that in my desperation, when I knew I was to be a mother soon, I confided all to Don Juan d'Alta, and by so doing perhaps saved my life and my child's."

Chapter XXIII. The Queen's Atonement

"Yes, but for the intervention of Don Juan d'Alta, my Chancellor at that time," continued the old lady, "my life might have ended in despair.

"From the very first, although he did not tell me so then, he saw that I had been simply *exploited* by this heartless and unprincipled scoundrel, Prince Adalbert of Rittersheim. But your father," she proceeded, turning to Dolores and placing her hand on hers, "your father, my dear, by his self-sacrifice and the pure affection which he bore me, saved me.

"He realised that he had to do with a villain whose object was plunder, and who at that time dominated the situation. He foresaw that a liberal outlay of money was the only thing that would rid me of this fiend. He went to Prince Adalbert and simply asked him his price.

"He named at first an exorbitant sum, *and the diamonds of my late father contained in the steel safe*.

"This was refused. Don Juan at last brought him to his knees by defying him and telling him to do his worst.

"Then he agreed to a yearly pension of one hundred thousand dollars, which would be paid to him on condition that he left me unmolested.

"He made a fight for the custody of the child which was coming, as I doubt not he thought that he could have a greater hold over me if he had it, but this request was flatly refused, and he sailed away from Aquazilia the richer by a great income, but bought at the price of a loving woman's happiness."

The old queen stopped and wiped the tears from her eyes.

"Do not go on, your Majesty," urged Dolores, half dazed at the disclosures; "you distress yourself."

The old lady brightened at once and pressed her hand, putting away her handkerchief.

"No," she answered; "I prefer to tell you *all* and *now*.

"By the aid of Don Juan and the Baroness d'Altenstein, who was broken down with grief at the course affairs had taken, my condition was concealed, and arrangements were made for my accouchement under circumstances of the greatest secrecy. Don Juan had abandoned all hope from the outset of legitimatising the child; his one object was to conceal my shame. This he succeeded in doing. I gave birth to a boy, and my love for him has been the great solace of my life."

"And he is living, madame?" I ventured to ask.

"Yes, living," she answered, the sweet smile playing about her lips again – "living, and the greatest comfort God has given me in my trials.

"From his babyhood he was the one thought I had; his training, his education, the fostering of good in his receptive mind that he might grow up a good man. And he has repaid me a thousandfold.

"But in those years great troubles came upon me. Prince Adalbert, known as one of the greatest roués and spendthrifts in Europe, had succeeded his father two years after he left me, and was now Grand Duke. His first wife had been taken back again – or he never could have faced his people – and had borne him a son. This son was fated to be the scourge of my life hereafter.

"Meanwhile, in the throes of a continental war, the Grand Duchy of Rittersheim was absorbed into the neighbouring great state, and the Grand Duke Adalbert, deposed and impoverished, became simply a pensioner, and a most importunate blackmailer of myself.

"His one great object in life – and later he confided this secret, with the story of our marriage, to his son – was to obtain possession of the great fortune in diamonds, still locked in the steel safe bequeathed me by my father, and which I had steadfastly refused to part with, nay, even to withdraw a single stone from.

"But the value had, in the drink-distorted mind of the Grand Duke Adalbert, become immensely exaggerated. The safe was believed by his son Waldemar to contain diamonds to the value of five millions of English pounds!"

Hence his intense rapacity in later years; for when my boy was twenty-five his father, the Grand Duke Adalbert, died, and was succeeded in the title only, for the power was gone, by his son Waldemar, but two years younger than my own.

"This Waldemar appears to have been evilly disposed from boyhood, and embittered against mankind in general, first by the loss of his Duchy, and in addition by the destruction of an eye which he suffered in some low fracas, for his delight was to mingle and drink with the lowest of mankind. On his father's death he came to Valoro and demanded that the pension paid to the late Duke by me should be continued to him!

"This was refused.

"Then he had the impudence to try and bargain with me, offering to keep silence for a certain sum. Finally he laid claim to the diamonds in the steel safe, which he stated were his father's property. My answer to his requests and fraudulent claims was to have him placed on board a steamer bound for Europe.

"Then he threatened me with his life-long vengeance. Leagued with a professional agitator named Razzaro, he commenced to undermine my authority with great subtilty, till in the end my simple people who once had loved me and my family grew to hate me, and to look upon Waldemar, even the Royalists, as a much-wronged person.

"You know the rest; it is written in the history of the world. My people rose in rebellion. I was dethroned, and with one single faithful companion, the Baroness d'Altenstein, fled to Europe in the warship of a friendly nation.

"But before the storm burst I had sent to Europe the steel safe and its precious contents, the diamonds.

"For some reasons, I have many times since

wished that it had sunk to the bottom of the Atlantic.

"For years I lived in one of the fairest cities of Europe with my faithful d'Altenstein, and for those years the Duke Waldemar left me in peace, being, I suppose, occupied in some other villainy.

"But suddenly he commenced his importunities again, and made one dastardly attempt, through others, to steal the safe from the bankers' vaults in which it lay, but this was frustrated.

"Harried to death by his persecution, I consulted a learned English judge whom I met in Society in Paris, Sir Henry Anstruther, your father," she added, turning to me, "and it has always seemed to me a providential coincidence that in my need I should also have turned to you.

"I asked this good English judge, without disclosing my secret, what he considered the most effectual mode for a woman to adopt to hide herself entirely from the world and her friends. I said I was very curious to know what his long experience had taught him in that respect.

"He seemed amused at my question, and thought for some time before replying, little guessing what was running in my mind. He answered me at last, and said that he thought that a person could be best hidden and lost to the world by living just a fairly ordinary life in a quiet way in one of the larger towns in England. That was his experience during his long life as a lawyer.

"I treasured his opinion, and formed a scheme in my mind upon it.

"Just then poor Carlotta d'Altenstein, a widow without friends, my dear companion, was seized with her mortal illness, and then I saw my scheme complete before me.

"By the lavish use of money, of which I had more than I needed by far, for my father's private fortune invested in Europe was very great, I contrived that I should change places with the Baroness d'Altenstein.

"To the public it was *I* who was ill; to the world at large, even to Don Juan, it was *I* who died. It was then that, passing as the Baroness d'Altenstein – in England as plain Mrs. Carlotta Altenstein – I went to the city of Bath, which had been recommended, and also offered certain devotional advantages to me, for I intended to give the remainder of my life to religion and the poor.

"There in Monmouth Street, where you saw me, Mr. Anstruther, amusing myself with philanthropic literature, I succeeded for ten years in hiding myself from the Duke Waldemar of Rittersheim, who had in a manner reformed himself and become a philanthropist too, *in public*; in secret his life was worse than ever. In that little room in which you found me, I was foolish enough to keep the steel safe, hidden away in a receptacle cut in the stone wall of the house. But the safe no longer contained all the diamonds. I had been gradually selling them and devoting the proceeds to the poor of the world. This convent, a refuge for aged men and women, and orphaned children, was founded with part of the money.

"But to my horror, at the end of the ten years, I met the Duke Waldemar, face to face, coming out of the Pump Room at Bath, where quietly and unobtrusively I had gone to take the waters. That was on the morning of the day I spoke to you, for I knew then that my refuge was a refuge no longer.

"I intended on the morrow to have asked you to help me remove what remained of the diamonds to a place of security and leave the safe behind. Perhaps I might have even encroached on your kindness to have asked you to escort me here, but it was arranged otherwise.

"During the night and early morning, I became aware that something was taking place in the next house, which up to then had stood empty. I connected it in my mind with some plot of the Duke, who I doubted not had had me followed home. The sequel proved I was right.

"This fear so worked upon me that, towards morning, I rose and commenced to write the letters to you and Don Juan, and to make them up in packets.

"The letter to the latter, in which I told him I should come here if I lived, of course I placed in the ebony casket with something else that was worth more to me than all the diamonds in the world; it was the certificate of my marriage to Prince Adalbert of Rittersheim at the little church of the remote mountain village in Aquazilia.

"I was far more fearful of losing that than all my fortune. It was the certificate of my honour and my son's birthright. I knew that if the Duke Waldemar once got it into his possession he could demand any price from me for its return.

"It was late in the morning, a dull foggy November morning, when I had finished sealing the packets and locked them away in the steel safe with my own key. The one I had given you was the only duplicate in existence; they both bore my father's initial C, he was Carlo the Third of Aquazilia.

"Having left directions on a paper which you could see within the safe when you opened it, I carefully locked it and hid my own key under a special place in the carpet.

"I intended then to write to you at once and tell you to come and open the safe, whatever might happen to me, for I believed that its hiding-place would not easily be discovered, but I never had this chance.

"Exhausted with want of sleep, I went back to my room and threw myself on my bed, half dressed as I was, with my white silk dressing-robe on in which I had sat writing half the night.

"I at once fell asleep and must have slept for hours, for it was dark again when I awoke, and then I was called back to consciousness by having my arm roughly shaken. I found the Duke Waldemar and two other men in my room.

"He at once demanded to know the whereabouts of the steel safe with the diamonds, and held a naked knife to my throat to force me to tell him.

"Life was of very little value to me in comparison with the needs of the poor for whom I was determined to preserve the riches.

"Each time I refused to tell him he pressed the knife closer to my throat, until it cut into the flesh, and I felt the warm blood trickling down on to my white dressing-robe.

"When he and his companions had been there it seemed to me a long, long time, and it was useless for me to shriek for help, I gave myself up for lost, turning my thoughts as well as I could to the next world.

"It was then that the Duke and his men were startled by hearing you open the front door of the house and stumble through the dark passage.

"With horrible curses they fled through the window.

"Then you came, and I had just the strength left to whisper to you to open the safe when I fainted away.

"I have no recollection of what occurred after. Many hours must have elapsed before I regained consciousness, and then I came to myself in an underground room of what I knew after to be a lonely tower on the hills near Bath."

"What, not Cruft's Folly?" I suggested.

"Yes," she replied thoughtfully; "I believe that was the name I afterwards learned was given to the place.

"I was waited on by a German woman, the wife of one of the Duke's followers, a big dark man with a black beard.

"My dress, my bed, and general surroundings were those of a poor country woman.

"But this black-bearded German and his wife were the means of saving me.

"There had been an accident, a man had fallen off the tower and been killed.

"The big dark man and his wife were terribly frightened, and in this state could not withstand the temptation of the big bribe I promised them if they would obtain my release.

"They brought a country cart to the tower, full of straw, as soon as it was dusk on the day of the accident, and in this I was driven to Devizes. From there I telegraphed to my bankers and they sent a special messenger to me with an abundance of money and a new cheque-book; from that time forth I was my own mistress again.

"The wound in my neck, which was only skin deep, had been carefully bandaged by the German woman; under the hands of a skilled doctor and nurse, it soon healed.

"I have very little doubt but that the Duke intended to keep me a prisoner in the tower until I disclosed the whereabouts of the diamonds.

"The big German who had arranged my escape – and to whom I gave five hundred pounds – told me that a grave had already been dug to receive my body in the old graveyard behind the house in Monmouth Street.

"Had the Duke discovered the diamonds, I should have been murdered to save further trouble from me; he knew, of course, I was already dead to the world. As it was, they only buried my blood-stained bed-linen in the grave when they carried me off from the house, after you had left the Duke stunned."

I could have told the old Queen that the big German did not long enjoy her five hundred pounds, but that he himself filled the grave intended for her, and which, probably, he had helped to dig. I did not tell her this, she had had trouble enough; but I had little doubt that the Duke had discovered that the man had played him false, and had shot him and disposed of his body in that way.

Queen Inez paused, and passed her frail white hand across her eyes.

"I have told you all now, I think," she said slowly, for she was fatigued. "When I was well enough I came here and found a telegram from Don Juan. I knew you had delivered the casket. Here I have remained; here I shall, if it be God's will, remain to the end."

Seeing that the long relation had tired her, I leant forward and filled one of the little liqueur glasses with the golden Chartreuse and handed it to her. She took it from me with a smile, and insisted that we should take some too. We sat sipping the delicious liqueur in silence, our gaze fixed on the blue lake and the white sails slowly moving in the stillness of the afternoon heat.

As I saw the colour returning to the Queen's face, I ventured to ask her another question.

"There is one person, madame," I said, "who's history you have not yet thought fit to tell us. Forgive me if I am presumptuous in asking the question. It is your son I speak of."

A very sweet smile came over her face as I ceased speaking. She glanced, it appeared involuntarily, at the sparkling liqueur in her little glass.

"My dear son's history is soon told," she said, still smiling. "He has been a Carthusian monk, a Trappist, since his youth. He never had the least inclination for the life of the world. He is the abbot of the monastery of San Juan del Monte, near Valoro."

Then I recollected his fair face, and blue eyes, and remembered that he had reminded me of *some one*; now I knew who that some one was – his mother. It was plain to me why Don Juan had taken us there.

"Every year," continued Queen Inez, "by the special permission of the head of his order, he comes to me and stays ten days. Those are, to me, ten days stolen from heaven. Thank God, he comes next month, and each time he comes," she added, with a smile, raising her little glass, "he brings me a present from his monastery of the veritable Chartreuse."

We lingered with the dear old Queen until the sun was declining over the lake, whose waters were turning a darker blue; the sister came with wraps and a warning glance to take her to her rooms in the convent.

At her request, during our short stay at Lucerne, we visited her again and again, until the day of parting came, and we bade her farewell on the terrace where we had first met her, above the blue waters of the lake.

There were tears in her eyes and ours when we left her, and the tears came back again to ours as we looked wistfully up at the terrace as Fritz rowed us away, and we saw her waving to us no longer.

That was the last we saw of her, or shall ever see in this world, for six months after we received a letter from the Reverend Mother telling us that "Madame la Comtesse" was dead, and Dolores and I, remembering her sufferings, her patience, and her great love, are presumptuous enough to think that heaven has gained another saint.

* * * * *

No, neither Ethel nor St. Nivel are married yet, but I would not say that they never will be. I have heard rumours of a Guardsman on the one hand, and a sweet Irish girl on the other.

At any rate, during those happy autumn weeks which Dolores and I invariably spend at dear old Bannington in the shooting season, if, by any chance, Ethel and I meet in the gloaming in the long, oak-panelled corridors, we indulge in no more cousinly kisses; she *won't*.

www.ingramcontent.com/pod-product-compliance
Lightning Source LLC
Chambersburg PA
CBHW020557030726
47497CB00007B/1976